It is true that you
can find a pot of gold at
the end of a rainbow.

Dedication

Freedom comes at a great price.

This book is dedicated to every soldier who has ever fought for this country to maintain our freedom, risking everything they have to ensure I can walk through my day, practicing my faith and living as every person desires - FREE.

May God Bless America

Chapters

Gravity
A SHORT Story

Jessica Schaub

Stretching to New Heights

"Families are like fudge--mostly sweet with a few nuts."
-Author Unknown

"Jeff!" my brother called from the hall. "Mom says to eat breakfast now. If we miss the bus again, she's going to make us walk."

I didn't answer because George would know where I was and what I was doing.

The door of my closet swung open and he laughed. "You seriously think that's going to help?"

I let go of the bar and dropped to the floor. "It might."

"Jeff, you're short. It's no *big* deal."

I tried to shove him out of the way with my shoulder as I walked by, but he towers over me and is twice as thick. Instead of shoving him I fell backwards into my laundry basket and he laughed again. "Is this why you've been eating so much spinach?"

"It's healthy. You should try it." I didn't tell him that I had read a report that kids who ate more vegetables were taller and stronger. Since frozen spinach was buy-one-get-two-free, mom bought frozen spinach and was thrilled that I ate it when she cooked it.[1]

---

[1] But even when it's cooked with onions and soy sauce, spinach still tastes like dirt.

George flexed his arms and his stupid biceps nearly shredded his t-shirt. He wears his shirts a size too small so he looks more muscular. "I don't think you need spinach. Just protein." He lowered his arms and reached a hand out to help me out of the basket. "Seriously, Jeff. Try protein. It tastes better and it works."

I batted his hand away, and he shrugged and left. "Don't be late. It's bad enough to have to ride the bus."

By the time I came downstairs, mom had washed the dishes and my cold spinach omelet was still in the pan.

"Change of plans," she said. "I can work a double shift today. Then I have a meeting tonight at church. We are organizing the food for the backpacks for Elmherst Elementary. I'll be home late."

"Again?" I asked.

"My mother worked, too," she said as she poured coffee into her travel mug. "I know the sacrifices you make because I'm gone at night.[2] It's this family's mission to help those who can't help themselves."

My dad mumbled something about her minimum wage job and her volunteering hours. I know Mom heard him because her face grew a shade of reddish-purple that meant she agreed with him, but was trapped by the tradition her mother had started and the situation they found themselves in when the economy tanked and took Dad's business down with it. My grandmother had been the president of every volunteer organization created and as a result established in her children a sense of duty to the less fortunate. The problem was that we were becoming one of the less fortunate.

---

[2] She is referring to the dishes I will have to do before I can finish my homework.

Art Class

"The artist who aims at perfection in everything achieves it in nothing." -Eugene Delacrois

"Mr. Stanhope," Mrs. Spaglio called me to the front of the art studio.[3] "I'm still waiting for your project proposal for the eighth grade ceiling tile competition."

"I'm still working on it."

"The school year is going to come to an end before you know it. It would be sad indeed if you left this school without leaving a mark."

I knew she was talking about my ceiling tile project, but I couldn't help feeling that she was addressing my overall average-ness.

"I'll work on it more this weekend."

She smiled. "Good. You are a fine artist. I'm looking forward to seeing your tile unveiled."

At our school, each eighth grader paints a ceiling tile. It's the mark we leave for upcoming students to look up

---

[3] It's really just a classroom outfitted with large tables stained with paint and markers, but Mrs. Spaglio insists we call it a *studio*. I wish every classroom had a different name. Science would be the Laboratory. English...the Library. I wonder how different the classrooms would seem if they just had a different name?

to[4]; a statement of what we believe, what we like, who we are.

The art teacher, Mrs. Spaglio,[5] had a crazy idea years ago that the eighth grade students would paint a ceiling tile as part of their final art contribution to the school. Mr. Retsim, the principal, loved the idea. The ceiling tiles were already paid for. The only expense would be the paint.

The custodian, Mr. Moppet, hates it. He spends hours each week climbing up the ladder to pull out a ceiling tile and carefully balance it as he climbs down. He dropped one once and the mess it made upset Mr. Retsim, who knew that the budget would be off because of the cost to replace it.[6] More than that, Mr. Retsim doesn't like the gaping holes in the ceiling while each tile is being painted, so Mr. Moppet needs to constantly change them out.

The ladder is his other nemesis.

"Can't leave the ladder out, Mr. Moppet," Mr. Retsim said. "It's a hazard for these young ones. Never know who might climb up into the ceiling to make a break for it."[7]

That's why it's common to see Mr. Moppet carrying the ladder like some overgrown child. He mutters to it,

---

[4] Literally.

[5] We, of course, call her Mrs. Spaghetti due to the fact that her hair is long and blonde and twisted into thick dreadlocks that look like cooked noodles, but never to her face. Byron Homes did that once and is still cleaning toilets after school every Wednesday and Thursday.

[6] Mr. Moppet and the Unfortunate Ceiling Tile. This sounds like a bad title to a book.

[7] No one knows for sure, but its statements like these that have led all of us to believe that Mr. Retsim was formerly a prison warden...or a prisoner.

complaining about the tiles and the students.[8]

This art project is my chance to succeed at something my brother and sister failed. George and Amelia's ceiling tiles are tucked away in the corner over the emergency exit in the science hallway. If I can win the ceiling tile competition, my tile will be hung over the door to the main office, I will get an 'A' in art, and I will be guaranteed a place in the advanced art class in high school, a class reserved for sophomores and juniors.

I know what you're thinking. Do I have any artistic ability? Compared to my brother and sister, I'm a Picasso. No, Picasso's work was too abstract. I'm more like Van Gogh. But compared to Caitlin Amore, I draw as if I have two left hands and paint like I have a brush in my mouth.[9] Caitlin Amore will be famous someday for her art work. She's my main competition for the main office tile prize.

She's also my next door neighbor and best friend.

---

[8] Mr. Moppet is not allowed to carry the ladder in the halls between classes anymore. That's how Cecilia Bunkle got her dentures.

[9] I realize some people can paint with a paintbrush in their mouth. I can't.

Government Class

"I don't care how poor a man is; if he has family, he's rich."
-M*A*S*H*

Mrs. Swen had a headache today and assigned the following: "Write a list of how a current event is affecting you personally."

My completed assignment:

How the Economy Ruined My Life

1.   My dad's business has lost 85% of its income. He is now the only employee and doing the work of three people.
2.   We sold our backyard play-set[10] and put in a garden. Now our summer vacation consists of tilling, planting, weeding, harvesting and canning.
3.   Having a garden means pulling weeds and eating vegetables. Corn on the cob – good. Okra – bad!
4.   My mom went back to work, which means that we all take turns making dinner and washing dishes, both of which cut into my TV and homework time.
5.   After a few months, the TV thing wasn't a

---

[10] We are all too old for it, but it was still sad to see it go.

problem anymore. My parents canceled cable. Now all have are the movies we didn't sell in the yard sale.

6. We shop at grocery stores where you have to bag your own stuff.

7. We clip coupons.

8. My mom tried canning green beans. The pressure cooker exploded, leaving the pressure gauge stuck in the ceiling. My dad left it there as a reminder that everything will sooner or later reach a boiling point.

9. My brother, my sister and I are the only kids in the school who don't have cell phones. Well, there is one cell phone for the three of us, but it's a pre-paid phone and we can't text on it without risking losing our bathroom privileges. We use it for when one of us is away from home and might need the phone. And because my older brother drives and my older sister has so many after school activities, one of them is usually in possession of the phone.

10. Because I never have the phone and never text, I don't know the acronyms for texting. Kids in my school can't text in class, so they speak with texting words, like OMG! when something unbelievable happens, or WTH? which has a swear word in it but isn't as bad as the version that my brother uses.

If Parents Were Once Our Age, Why Don't They Understand the Seriousness of the Issue?

"We build too many walls and not enough bridges."
-Isaac Newton

"So what's the big deal?" dad asked. "It's just a ceiling tile. George and Amelia didn't stress out about it."

"Dad! It's not just a ceiling tile," I said, "it's the artistic representation of my legacy."

Dad looked at me over the rim of his bifocals. "A legacy on a ceiling tile. I think I need more information."

"Every eighth grader paints something on a ceiling tile and it's put up in the school for everyone to see. It has to be perfect."

"George and Amelia painted tiles. Are they still up?"

"Yeah. Over by the exit doors in the science wing." I didn't tell him that those doors were only used during fire drills or if someone mixed the wrong chemicals together and we needed to evacuate the school. That's how bad their tiles were. That's how the Stanhope name gained a bad reputation in art. I have a shot to change that; to win at something George and Amelia never had a chance to win.

"And how long does this ceiling tile stay up?" Dad

8

asked.

"Forever!" I yelled. He just wasn't getting the importance of the ceiling tile dilemma.

Dad set down his newspaper and took an interest in the problem. "What can you paint well?"

I shrugged. "I'm pretty good at trees and stone walls. Animals are pretty easy."

"Sounds like your problem is solved. Paint a tree in front of a stone wall." Satisfied, dad picked up his newspaper again.

"No, Dad. That's stupid. Who's going to care about some old tree and a wall?"

"This wouldn't have anything to do with," dad asked, eyebrows raised, "a girl?"

"Not everything revolves around girls, dad."

"Really?" he asked, his smile was obvious even through the newspaper. "When I was your age, most things - important things - were either about girls or football."

"Caitlin likes teddy bears." I leaned forward. Even my dad, the king of practicality must understand this. "There's no way I'm going to paint a teddy bear."

Dad leaned forward and took off his reading glasses. "That would take years to live down."

"Exactly."

"What else does she like?" he asked.

"I don't know." I've known Caitlin all my life and I know she likes teddy bears and chocolate chip cookies and letters in the mail. I know she wears Red, White and Blue on Fridays as a message of support for our troops when we don't have to wear school uniforms. She loves to camp and fish and, at times, acts more like a boy than a girl. But none of those things would come together in my mind as a painting that would both impress Caitlin *and* win the contest.

9

"Then that's your first task," Dad said, pointing at me with his glasses.

"What is?" I asked.

"Finding out what Caitlin likes."

"How?"

Dad shrugged and put his glasses back on. "That's up to you, buddy."

"Thanks, Dad." I left the room. I wanted to say 'Thanks for nothing', but that would have gotten me grounded. Now I knew what I needed to do and had no idea how to do it. I hoped Caitlin likes trees. I can paint trees.

Second-Hand Ideas

"To every action there is always opposed an equal reaction."
-Isaac Newton

Who knew that the decisions made in Washington D.C. would affect what I would wear in gym class? With the tanked economy, my parents had to tighten the budget. That, in turn, means that we don't buy steak for the Fourth of July, we shop at second-hand stores for clothes, and that we are on the lunch program at school. Kids whose parents can't afford to pay for the hot lunch program are given a red[11] lunch card pass, a discounted price for lunch, and a whole slew of new problems (being that all us red-card kids also are not expected to purchase the gym uniform).

Sigh.

That means a second-hand gym uniform.

Gross.

That means the clothes I have to wear everyday for gym class belonged to someone else last year.

Embarrassing.

Someone else sweated in those clothes all last year.

Disgusting.

---

[11] Red. Bright red. Like an alarm or a flashing banner screaming "The world is cruel!"

Just like the red lunch card, which declares me as a 'low-income' kid, my gym uniform has someone else's name on it. Across the chest of the t-shirt is a screen-printed rectangle in which the gym teacher writes your last name in permanent marker. I had hoped that when the t-shirts were washed, the name would fade, but my uniform hadn't been washed at all.

Repulsive.

The stench of last year's sweat from whoever 'Haan' was floated up from the yellow-stained armpits and curled my nose hairs.

Using duct tape, Mr. Pullup covered the name of the original owner of the shirt and wrote "Stanhope".

Yep. Nothing like a strip of duct tape across my chest to announce my second-hand needs.

My mom wrinkled her nose when I brought out my gym uniform.

"Don't they wash these before passing them on?" she asked as she lifted the lid of the washer for me to drop them in.

"You know, mom," I said, "a new uniform is only twenty dollars. I have that in my college fund. I don't mind taking it out."

"No." She poured a full cup of liquid detergent into the washer. "We don't want to get into the habit of pulling money from our savings account just to cover up a little pride. Once this is washed, it will be just fine."

I knew it was useless to argue. My mom, the money hound, wouldn't buy my sister a new retainer even after it had been thrown away and found among a pile of cold meatloaf and noodles in the trashcan. My sister refused to wear it, but mom ran it through the dishwasher and declared it completely sanitized.

My gym t-shirt endured heavy-duty stain remover soaked on the armpits overnight, a tad of bleach added to the wash machine to rid it of that sweat-stench, and two cycles before my mother declared it fit to wear. The shirt looked almost new – except for the duct tape, which didn't survive the washings. But as we pulled off the wet tape, the permanent marker underneath had faded and with a bit of careful writing, I was able to write "Stanhope" to cover up "Haan".

"Good as new," my mother smiled as she admired our work.

George walked by and nodded. "Not bad, mom. Wonder how much you just spent in water and electricity to get it to look new?"

Mom shot him a look that meant, *You are two words away from missing dinner* and George muttered a sulky apology and left.

"I think it's great," mom said.

I did too.

There Is No Over the Rainbow

"Character is much easier kept than recovered."
- Thomas Paine

Every kid has something that they are good at, or so I'm told. It stands to reason that for everything someone excels at, there is something they are terrible at.[12] One of my current enemies is gym class. Every Tuesday and Thursday, we do Circuit Training.

It's torture.

I mean real, honest-to-God torture.

After roll call, we line up on red, orange, yellow, green, blue, purple or gold lines to indicate which level of circuit we are going to attempt to pass. Circuit training is a series of exercises that must be done in order and within a certain amount of time, and for short people like me the wall jumps pose a challenge.

Any third grader can do the red level, so I'm told, but it took me all of sixth grade to pass it. I have yet to pass the yellow level.

---

[12] Yes, I know I ended that in a preposition. How do you not end some sentences in a preposition? Should I write, "It stands to reason that for everything that someone excels in, there would be something at which they are terrible." OK, so I suppose that's exactly how it should be, but who talks like that?

Gold[13] is the highest level. It's so tough that the gym teacher only allows kids to attempt it once a month. This is mostly because Mr. Moppet cleans the gym floor once a month. Gold Circuit Challenge is always scheduled for that mopping day because someone always pukes.[14]

Here's what I tried today:

Push-ups. Yellow level (the level I'm trying to pass) is 20 pushups. Gold level is 50 pushups.

Stairs. For this, the bottom step of the bleacher is pulled out and we have to step up, making sure both heels are on the step and then step down again. Yellow: 15. Gold: 50.

Jump Rope. Yellow: 50 jump ropes with no misses. Gold: 300 but you can miss twice.

Wall jumps. Along the wall under the basketball score keeper are rainbow colored stripes. Red is the lowest and the Pot of Gold at the top of the rainbow is the highest. This is where being short is holding me back. The highest I can jump is to yellow. Blue is impossibly out of reach which makes the Gold line ridiculous. I might as well try to reach the clouds.

Pull-ups. Yellow: 3. Gold: 8.

Sit-ups. Yellow: 25. Gold: 65.

Sprinting. Each color level has a number. Red is 1, Orange is 2, and all the way up to Gold, which is 7. We run around the gym the number of times that match the level we are trying to pass. For example, Red runs once

---

[13] I'm sure you've figured this out – it's the rainbow and gold is the ultimate goal. It's at the end of the rainbow.

[14] There is a story that Mr. Moppet and Mr. Pullup don't like each other. I know the story behind it, but it's way too long for a footnote and involves some bad language and I'm not allowed to include it in this story.

around the gym; yellow: three times. Gold = 7 times around the gym!

The sprinting lane is closest to the bathrooms and most kids can make it to a toilet if they feel like lunch is revisiting. Some kids don't.

Circuit Training takes the entire class time to finish. We each have to partner up with someone and take turns running through the Circuit with one person doing the exercises and the other person counting.

Today is Thursday. I was partnered with Mike. According to his tally, I completed the Green level. I know I didn't because I counted, too. I did the Orange level. I was going for Yellow but I missed it with the wall jumps. I can only reach Orange. There's no way I did Green. But thanks to Mike reporting an erroneous tally to Mr. Pullup, I've moved up to Green.

Why is that so bad, you ask? I can't go back. Once a level has been completed, you have to work on the next level. Now, on Tuesday, I have to do Green. Not Orange, or Yellow, but Green. Do you know what that means?

It means I should have gone with my instinct and corrected Mike when he reported the wrong numbers. I didn't because I didn't want to embarrass him (he's not too smart with numbers). But now I'm going to suffer for it.

Who knew that one kid's math troubles would bring about another kid's failure in gym?

What Does OOTW Mean?

"There are big ships and small ships. But the best of all is friendship." - Author Unknown

News of my finally passing the Green level spread quickly through my incredibly small group of friends.

Mike, my circuit training counter, is my friend. So are Jabari and Alex. It's just the four of us.[15] We all have something that others find nerdy or stupid or irritating. Or all three. I'm small and easy to miss in a crowd. We are the un-cool kids and we know it. But all we have is each other and that's good enough.

Jabari has a glass eye. It was freaky when I first met him, but I'm used to it now. It fell out once in gym class. I thought that he could just pop it back in, but it had to be cleaned first and checked for damage. He missed the rest of the school day and I spent two lonely hours in Math and Language Arts, wishing I had a glass eye that could get me out of class.

Alex stutters and is autistic. We all know his quirks and can manage well. We all became friends last year with Alex when our homeroom teacher asked us to take him under our wings and give him support. I felt obligated to

---

[15] Caitlin is my friend too, but during the school day we stick with our other friends. I guess we are bus and afterschool friends.

help because our homeroom teacher, Miss Faith, is also a Religious Education teacher at St. John's Church. How could I say no to someone like that? We struggled with his autism at first, but his mom really helped us understand what's important to him and how we can help make his days smoother. He's a good guy; I am so used to him now, I sometimes forget he's Autistic.

Mike is brilliant when it comes to storytelling and remembering jokes, but socializing is his nemesis, so he sticks close to us. He's in the remedial Math class and has been tested several times for severe learning disabilities. So when Mike counted for me, he truly believed that I did Green level.

After gym class, I had Math and Science and then the bus ride home. That's when I realized that Mike had told Jabari and Alex about the Green circuit level.

"How'd you do it?" Jabari asked.

"Yeah," Alex said between bites of left over lunch, "L. . .l. . .l. . .last year it was all you c. . .could do to reach the r. . .red stripe on wall jumps!"

"Thanks." I wasn't thrilled to hear the lack of faith in my jumping abilities, no matter how grounded in truth they were. "But, I don't think—"

"OMG Jeff!" That was Amber's voice. "I heard about the Green circuit level. That's OOTW. I've been working on the green level, but I can't do the pull-ups," she said.

"Yeah, those are really hard," I said. "Just takes practice."[16]

She smiled and continued down the aisle of the bus to the back where all the kids with tons of friends sit. You know, the popular kids. Kids with class. Kids taller than five feet.

---

[16] That was true, and probably advice I should take.

18

Jabari eyed me with suspicion. "You really did it?"

I looked at Mike, who was smiling as if he'd just announced the winner of the Iron Man Triathlon to the whole world. "I wasn't really paying attention to counting and stuff.[17] I was just doing the best I could."[18]

"You're getting closer to an 'A' in gym. Closest you've ever been," Jabari said.[19]

"Thanks. What does OOTW mean?"

Jabari shook his head and laughed. "Out of this world."

At our bus stop, Caitlin and I walked home together.

"Next week there will be a cubby opening," she reminded me. "You might be next."[20]

"I hope not."

"Still don't have any ideas?"

I thought back to dad's idea about trees. But what's so special about a tree? "Not even one."

Amber, who was walking behind us, laughed.[21] "OMG

---

[17] That was a lie.

[18] That was the truth.

[19] That would have been the truth if I had actually finished the Green level. Because next week I would have a new counting partner. Next week I will barely finish the Yellow level, like always. Next week my status as an athlete is over. Such a short-lived legacy
.

[20] In our art studio, the back of the room has been transformed with cubicle walls from an office that closed. There are four little rooms divided with these cubicle walls. Every two weeks, Mrs. Spaglio draws four names from a bowl and those students have that space to complete their ceiling tile. Caitlin had already finished hers last month: an almost perfect copy of VanGogh's *Stormy Night*.

[21] ...or should I say LOL?

you two,[22] listen to this. Rachel and Sarah are on the bus."

"We know," Caitlin sighed. "We just got off that same bus."

Amber didn't hear her and continued. "Mr. Wolley missed a stop and that little sixth grader, you know the one with the purple bands on her braces? Well, she starts to COL[23] and Mr. Wolley was, like, nervous because that girl's mom gets mad so quick—you remember that day?[24] So he slammed on the brakes and a kid—I don't know who—that was standing up fell over and now has a bloody nose. TSA!"

"What's TSA?" I asked Caitlin.

"That's so awesome."

Amber continued texting with Rachel and I wondered if she even cared if we had heard her.

We stopped at the mailboxes. Our neighborhood was designed to keep traffic low; there is only one way in and out, so there are no short cuts to anywhere by driving through these streets. The school buses aren't permitted in, so we are all dropped off at the main entryway and walk home from there. The mailboxes are near the entryway; all 67 green boxes lined up like soldiers, each with the address in white numbers on the door. Even the mailman doesn't drive down our street.

There was nothing exciting about the mail for me. My birthday is in the summer, so there were no cards for me,

---

[22] She said "two" but I really think in her mind she said "2". What's the difference, you ask? It's just a hunch that Amber sees everything she says because she texts more than she speaks.

[23] I'm assuming that's 'cry out loud'.

[24] "That day" is referring to a day when Mr. Wolley didn't have this little sixth grader with purple bands on her braces on the bus, because she boarded the wrong bus at school. Her mother was furious and yelled at him in front of everyone.

and no one sends letters by snail mail anymore. No one, except John Paul. That's why Caitlin loves the mail; it holds the possibility for letters from her brother who is serving a tour in Iraq. There were four letters from John Paul today. They come in groups like that because the mail where he's stationed is only collected once a week.

"Does he still email?" I asked. "It would seem so much easier and faster to just use computers."

"Yeah. Last weekend we Skyped with him."

"So why does he still send letters?"

Caitlin smiled. "Because he knows I check the mail every day. He can write just to me. Mom and dad email with him, but he writes to me."

"My brother would never send me a letter in the mail."

"He would if he was in the war. John Paul told me in a letter that most of the soldiers write. They don't always have a computer, but they can all carry paper and pen."

"My brother would probably send me pressed spiders or a dead scorpion. You know, something that really says how he feels about me. George's nick-name for me isn't nice, either. John Paul calls you Kit-Kat."

"And only John Paul can call me that," Caitlin reminded me. She didn't really like other people calling her after a candy bar, but John Paul could.

"I would never try to be John Paul," I said. "Even though his jokes aren't over my head, everything else about him is."

Laughing, Caitlin opened the first letter after sorting them.[25]

"How is he?" I asked.

"Good. He says that their nights are cooler and that

_____

[25] As John Paul puts each letter in an envelope, he puts the date in the lower left corner. Caitlin reads them in chronological order.

his patrols are pretty uneventful."

"That's good."

"Very good. He says to say 'hi' to you and asks if we could send more chocolate chip cookies. Do you have time today?"

"We have an algebra test tomorrow. Let's study while the cookies bake."

Three hours later, the cookies were cooled and packaged with more notebook paper and pens, three Kit-Kat bars and a few pictures Caitlin took of the yard so John Paul could see the greening of the trees. "I'll mail it on my way to work," Mr. Amore said.

"Wait!" Caitlin added a few teddy bear stickers to the package. "That way he knows it's from me."

Mrs. Amore came into the kitchen and tied on an apron. "Time for dinner prep."[26]

"See you tomorrow." I snagged one more cookie on my way out the door.

I thought a lot about John Paul that night and how a simple batch of chocolate chip cookies would mean so much to him. He didn't ask for them in every letter, which led me to think that there were moments when spirits needed lifting and homemade cookies were the answer.

That was John Paul, he always loved the little things. When Caitlin and I were younger, John Paul would

---

[26] Mrs. Amore doesn't allow people to see her house unless it is perfect. John Paul always said it was because she was a Real Estate Agent and had heard all kinds of judgments passed on families during open houses. She takes no such risk. She prefers to be thought of as tidy and in control. Her house was a mirror image of that.

babysit us. Their parents would go out for the evening and I would be invited over to play. He was unlike any babysitter I ever had—he actually played with us. Monopoly, Life, Sorry, tag, bloody murder.[27]

He is a great story teller. Caitlin and I would give him three key words and he could make up a story that would have us either hysterical with laughter or afraid of every dark corner. Of all the older kids in our neighborhood, I know him the best. He's approachable and fun with a splash of mystery. There is only one thing about him that he never told anyone: on his cheek and chin there is a long scar. It happened when I was five and I remember that his dad said he should have stitches, but John Paul refused, saying that the scar would be more impressive without.

And it was.

The source of the scar remains a mystery. Even his parents don't know, despite all their questions.

---

[27] George and Amelia would join us at the park to play this. One time, Caitlin and Amelia screamed so loudly, a neighbor lady called the police. She calls the police all the time any noise startles her. Dad says that's because she lives alone.

23

Do All Bad Things Come in Threes?

"In some families, please *is described as the magic word. In our house, however, it was* sorry." *–Margaret Laurence*

Have you ever heard the expression, "Bad things come in threes?" My dad knows this well. He is not a superstitious man, but after today he might start carrying a rabbit's foot. Mom picked us up from school and drove us to the junk yard where dad stood staring at his beloved Volvo. It was sad. He bought that car right after college, before he and mom were married. He bought it used and he loved it. And now it was dead.

George pulled on mom's sleeve as we approached. "How long has he been standing there?"

"A while." Mom walked up and put her arm around dad.

I've written this moment in play format, that way my assignment for English class is finished.

CHARACTERS:
MOM: Wearing her work clothes, smelling of coffee, bacon and eggs, and looking tired.

DAD: Wearing jeans and a sweatshirt, in a state of defeat.

GEORGE, AMELIA, & JEFFERSON: children to

24

MOM and DAD, all fresh from school and anxious to just go home.

SETTING:
Junkyard; standing in front of newly crashed Volvo, once the pride and joy of DAD.

MOM
I just don't understand how this happened.
DAD
The tree did most of the damage.
MOM
How did you run off the road?
DAD
The tire blew and it pulled hard to the right. I managed to miss another car, but the tree refused to move out of the way.

MOM
I thought you were working all day. Where were you going?

DAD
To the mall.

MOM
Why?

DAD
To replace my cell phone.

MOM
Why?

DAD
Because I dropped it in the sink.

MOM
(Didn't say anything, but the expression on her face clearly said, "Explain yourself!")

DAD

(sighs)

I forgot it was in my hand when I reached for a cup of soapy water.

MOM

(Same expression on her face)

DAD

The soapy water was to put out the fire.

MOM

What fire?

DAD

The microwave fire. There must have been a little piece of foil on my lunch plate. I left the kitchen to make a phone call and when I came back fire was springing out of the microwave and up the cabinets.

MOM

(MOM covers her forehead with her hand and shakes her head.)

How much damage?

DAD

Oh, not much. Just blackened some of the wood. And melted a section of the countertop. The curtains. Most of the spice containers.

MOM

I think I'm going to be sick.

DAD

(Puts his arm around MOM and sighs)

I can't believe it. I thought she'd run forever.

MOM

She was a good car.

(All characters stand together staring at the car)

GEORGE

It doesn't look that bad. All I see is a dented hood and missing muffler. How can it be totaled?

DAD

Most of the damage was internal. Life-threatening injuries.

(George and Jefferson exchange exasperated looks. Amelia was as emotional as DAD.)

DAD

(Blowing his nose loudly into a tissue.)

I remember the day I bought you. You had that little key scratch under the lock. It was freezing cold and you were the only car that started. You never let me down. All three of my children were safe within your seat belts. Thank you, old gal. It's been a good haul.

(He pats the hood lovingly.)

JEFFERSON

(Closes his eyes and shakes his head.)

Oh, please don't.

DAD

Let's go around and share a favorite memory.

JEFFERSON

(Sighs)

You did.

We all did. And I actually had a lump in my throat. Mom cried too, but I think her tears were more from the fact that we were now a one-car, microwave-free, burnt-kitchen, no cell phone insurance family.

To Lie or Not to Lie?

"It is curious—curious that physical courage should be so common in the world, and moral courage so rare." –Mark Twain

"Mike, I can't do the Blue level," I told him on Tuesday after gym class. I did finish Yellow but was a far cry from Green.

"You did Green last time."

Here is was. The moment of truth. "No. I didn't."

Mike frowned. "Yes you did. I counted."

"I counted, too. I did Yellow. I was almost to Orange except for pull-ups and wall jumps."

Mike thought about what I had said for a moment and shrugged his shoulders. "You'll thank me," he said, grinning as if he'd handed me all my dreams on a silver platter instead of my own severed head.

"How? What good could possibly come from this?"

Mike threw his gym clothes in his locker. "You need an "A" in gym. I just got it for you."

"By lying?"

"*I* didn't lie. Look, if you don't want the A, tell Mr. Pullup that you lied. If you want a shot at an "A" and a chance to try out for any sport in high school as a freshman, you need this."

He had a point—all high school try outs for freshman are only open to those who get an "A" in junior high gym

28

class; particularly eighth grade gym class. Mike knew I wanted to play on the high school golf team.[28]

"I just don't think it's right," I argued. "You need to tell him you miscounted."

"No way!" Mike turned on me, his taller frame taking every intimidating advantage. "I'm already in the dumb class for math. If they find out, they'll send me to the special ed. programs. I'll be the subject of every Tweet for a month! You can't do that to me!"

"And if I can't even finish the Green level at the next Circuit Challenge I'll fail gym class and won't be able to play golf next year."

Mike shrugged. "One year. Big deal. You can play the next year. If I'm found out, I'll be in special ed. programs forever."

"Do you have any idea how impossibly difficult it is to make the team as a sophomore?"

Mike slammed his locker door shut. "I'll pull some strings and work it out to be your partner again at the challenge. It will be fine. Trust me." He flung his empty backpack over his shoulder and left.[29]

Standing there, watching him walk away, I envisioned my dad's face when he saw an "A" on my report card for gym. He might smile and pat me on the shoulder and look at me differently, like I was stronger or taller or worthy of something. But if something went wrong, if Mike wasn't my partner and I didn't even finish the

---

[28] Yes, even carrying your own clubs and walking 9 to 18 holes requires an A in 8th grade gym, which means passing at least the blue circuit level, which according to Mike was only possible for me through a lie.

[29] Mike thinks it unreasonable for teachers to assign homework. His parents support this opinion. That could explain a great deal about Mike and his math troubles.

Orange level – I would be a freshman caddy, lugging golf bags for kids with friends who could count.

Is It Really Goodwill?

"The real measure of your wealth is how much you'd be worth if you lost all your money." —Author Unknown

When I got home, mom threw a sandwich at me and said, "Time to shop for new clothes."

"Again?" I asked.

"George's ankles are showing. I'm sure your shoes are too small but you never take the time to notice. Your sister is coming along because she won't be left out of a shopping trip."

"That's a change," I said, referring to the end of summer clothes shopping trip. At the beginning of the school year, my mom rallied to buy us all new clothes for school; it's been an annual tradition since George started kindergarten. But it came to a screeching halt this year.

Mom and Dad sent us kids into the other room for hours while they poured over the budget.[30] The kitchen table was piled with dad's expense spreadsheet, pencils, calculator, and coffee. They crunched numbers, cut

---

[30] At first, being sent away seemed like a ticket to do what we wanted, which we did. But it also meant that the kitchen was closed to snacks and then dinner because of the "Budget Meeting". By the time it was over, we couldn't even order a pizza because they were so adamant that we not spend the extra money. We had left overs, again, enhanced with a new round of ground beef.

31

expenses, and trimmed the savings account. After the "Budget Meeting" mom announced that school shopping would still take place because we were growing.

What we realized as we pulled into a parking lot was that we weren't shopping at a department store or at the mall; we were at a second-hand consignment store. My sister refused to buy anything second-hand because according to her, anything in this store probably belonged to girls from school and how could she possibly go to school in her friends old clothes. My mom agreed, stating that there was one more place we could go that had clothing and she could buy anything she wanted there. My brother and I shared a meaningful glance. We weren't about to fall under one of mom's "choose your own fate" traps.

Amelia hid behind the hanging clothes, trying to blend among the jackets and jeans.

"Don't you think that if anyone recognizes you, it would only be because they are shopping here, too?" George asked.

"There are windows," Amelia said. "Someone could walk by and see me in here. I could be buying *their* old clothes."

I glanced at the one window in the store. It was the window on the door and covered mostly by a white curtain; probably a second-hand curtain.

If I thought that Amelia was acting odd at the first store, when mom pulled into the parking lot of the second store, World War III broke out in the mini-van.

"NO! Mom! NO!" Amelia shouted, unbuckling her seat belt and sliding to the floor to cover her head with a shirt I had just bought. "Drive us out of here. Now!"

Mom kept her cool.[31] "Do you want clothes for school?"

"Not from Goodwill."

"It's here or nowhere."

"Why can't we just charge new clothes to the credit card?" Amelia whined. "Don't you understand what wearing old clothing will do to my reputation?"

"The credit card is not an option. And *you* are quickly running out of options. Do you want to buy clothes for school here, or are you ready to go home?"

Amelia, with tears streaking down her face, sighed. "Can we go back to the consignment shop?"

"It wasn't good enough for you a half hour ago. You were rude in the store and you've yelled at me in the car. What have you done to deserve a trip back to where we just were?" Mom asked.

"Nothing. I'm sorry, mom."

"Are we going into Goodwill or are we going home?" Mom asked again.

"Goodwill."

Amelia cried throughout her entire Goodwill shopping experience. She did find clothes, but when we got home, she washed them all twice and then set out to alter them to make them her own. She sewed buttons on the legs of her jeans and painted flower petals around them. She turned the long-sleeved shirts into short-sleeve shirts and converted a sweater into a jacket. Now, girls at Amelia's school are painting on their jeans and asking her to help them alter sweaters into coats and purses. A few people have even paid Amelia to do it for them.

"Are you going to use your money to go to the mall

---

[31] I think even parents enjoy a bit of revenge every now and then. Mom didn't even yell at Amelia for yelling at her.

and buy new clothes?" mom asked as she handed Amelia her sandwich.

Amelia laughed. "No. I like my new look. Besides, it turns out that other kids at school shop at consignment stores, too. I was thinking that I could take some of the painted jeans there to sell. It'd earn 50%!"

Who Would Dance With Me?

"Most of what is said under excitement is regretted when we become ourselves again." —James Lendall Basford

Every morning the eighth grade communications class does the announcements with Mr. Retsim. In the back of the auditorium, a small room has been outfitted with a cozy news desk, a camera, and a sound booth. The first hour communications class is for the kids who are in drama, win leading roles in every play, and walk down the hallways with a particular superiority that the rest of us find intimidating.[32]

This morning, Mr. Retsim appeared rather green on the screen a symptom he experiences often. Tom Fickle greeted the school. Cooper Jones did a fairly decent weather report. Amanda Freeder lead her group of friends through the "Do's and Don'ts of Fashion for Girls." And then the lead story was announced by Mr. Retsim:

"Good morning, ladies and gentlemen. I am Mr.

---

[32] And funny. The lead news caster is Tom Fickle. He's 6 feet tall and brags that he's already shaving. And I don't doubt it; his voice is as deep as my dad's. But we would never joke about it in front of him, or within earshot, or near one of his friends, or anywhere except Jabari's room. That would be like committing suicide. Tom Fickle can't stand to be teased.

Retsim, Principal of this fine school.[33] I'm here to invite you all to a special event taking place Saturday evening. A dance[34]. We will begin at 6:00 in the evening in the cafeteria. Dress codes will be strictly enforced.[35] Gentlemen are to wear pants without holes and shirts without graphics. Girls are to wear appropriate clothing which doesn't bare any skin of the navel[36] and skirts that are closer to the knees than the hips. All students will adhere to standard school rules in regards to behavior."

Tom Fickle piped in. "Thank you, Mr. Retsim. And to whom do we owe thanks for this special event?"

"The parents of the Athletic Boosters. They will be decorating the cafeteria as well as providing snacks."

Tom turned to the camera and spoke directly to the school, "You heard it here first, folks.[37] The dance admission is two dollars a person. And I believe the music is being provided by Theo Fickle."[38]

The noise in the hallway between classes was a constant roar for the rest of the day. Being Wednesday, there were only three days to make plans.

Boys asked girls to go with them to the dance.

Girls asked boys to go with them to the dance.

Several girls were seen running to the bathroom in

---

[33] duh.

[34] At this point, there was a collective gasp from the girls throughout the school and it felt as though all of the air had been completely sucked out of the atmosphere.

[35] At this point, every boy in the school moaned.

[36] The entire school giggled at this, and some girls glanced at each other and agreed to wear just such clothing.

[37] As if there is another in-school news program.

[38] Theo is Tom's much-older brother. He's in college and has enough speakers and lights to communicate with someone on the moon.

tears because the right boy didn't ask. Or worse, said 'No'.

Mike, Alex, Jabari and I didn't participate in all this. We knew we would go to the dance. We knew we wouldn't be dancing with any girls.

There is some comfort in not being popular and in knowing that it's just a waste of time to ask a girl to the dance. One "NO! OMG! NO!" will drive that fact home very quickly.

Do Current Events Include References From OMG.com?

"If you don't like how things are, change it! You are not a tree!"
—Jim Rohn

Do you have Current Events at your school? Current events can be defined as "the routine of submitting one victim a day to scouring the internet and watching the evening news in preparation for reporting to the class." Worse than watching the news with your parents is when you have to walk to the front of the class, turn and face everyone, and talk about something that is important, but not important to you.

My turn to report on the current events was today. I watched the news. I read the reports online. And you know what the biggest event was in our city? A kangaroo escaped from the zoo. It even made the National News.

That's it. A Kangaroo jumped the enclosure and ran (or bounced) for its life. No war reports, no Presidential tours.[39] But not for Jefferson Sherman Stanhope Jr. I get a runaway kangaroo.

Kangaroos are marsupials, which means that the

---

[39] Mrs. Swen is big on Presidential tours – so big that she'll take over for you and finish your current events report. And give you an A!

38

babies are raised in a pouch. How do I know that? Re-runs of Jack Hanna's Saturday morning safari show on channel 8 which is available with rabbit ear antennae, no cable required. Anyway, news of the runaway kangaroo stirred more than giggles from the girls in class. Maybe boys aren't supposed to think that marsupials are interesting or maybe we aren't supposed to know about pouches and stuff. I don't know. All I do know is that once Alison Whitmere started laughing, the other girls joined in and no one could stop. Mrs. Swen tried to stop them with a look, but that just added more fuel to the fire.

"Thank you, Jefferson," Mrs. Swen said, giving up on the current events report for today.

I slugged back to my seat and glared at Alison and her troop of gigglers.

What was so funny about kangaroos?

As it turns out, nothing.

The funny part was the long noodle of spaghetti left over from lunch that had attached itself to the front of my pants.

Cubby Call

"Life beats down and crushes the soul and art reminds you that you have one." —Stella Adler

"Mr. Stanhope," Mrs. Spaglio read my name off a strip of paper that she pulled from the jar. "It's your turn for a cubby. I hope you have your project planned."

"Not yet."

She tossed her hair back over her shoulder, almost hitting me in the face with it. "It's been two months since you've been told to begin preparing for it."

"I'm just having a really hard time deciding what to do."

"What are your passions?" she asked.

I honestly don't know. In fact, I feel nervous when a teacher asks me about what I like. I golf, and I enjoy it, but I'm not going to paint a golf scene. I like books. I suppose I could do something about that; maybe a bunch of characters floating out of a book? That might be good. The winners from the last two years both did copies of famous pieces. That seems to be a good rule to follow if you want to win, but I don't like the idea of copying someone else's work in order to win. If I do win this ceiling tile art contest, I want it to be because my work is original.

Mrs. Spaglio interrupted my thoughts. "I see you have

many ideas racing around in your mind. May I suggest that you start sketching some of them out? At least that way, the next time I call you up here, you'll have something to show for progress."

"Yes, ma'am."

"I'll put your name back in, but the next time, you will have to start."

Ever Have One of Those Days?

"When dealing with people, remember you are not dealing with creatures of logic, but creatures of emotion." –Dale Carnegie

Let's recap: There's a dance this weekend and I know I will go, but not dance. I still have no idea what to paint for the ceiling tile contest. Mike has tied me up in a lie that might result in my not playing golf next year in high school. I'm now being called "Spaghetti Boy" by Alison and her laughing troop. And then Caitlin and I missed the bus after school. It was Frank's fault. Here's how it all went down.[40]

SCENE ONE

CHARACTERS

JEFFERSON STANHOPE, JR.: eighth grade student; small for his age, short brown hair, wearing school uniform the way it's supposed to be worn (shirt tucked in).

FRANK DARING: big, hulky eighth grader who walks as if he is as wide as the hallway, has the beginnings of a mustache and needs to wear deodorant, but doesn't. Also wearing school uniform with shirt un-tucked and a

---

[40] I'm writing this as a play for another assignment for English class.

graphic t-shirt of a mildly inappropriate nature is visible underneath.

CAITLIN AMORE: fellow classmate, good friend of Jeff's. Also wearing school uniform and adhering to the rules of how it should be worn. Clothing is perfectly ironed and clean. Long reddish hair is neatly combed. Freckles. Cute.

SETTING:

Center stage is Jefferson at his locker, trying to pack 50 pounds of textbooks into a backpack certified to hold only 30. Enter FRANK, who shoves a small six-grader out of the way before stopping to torment Jeff.

FRANK

(He leans on Jeff's locker door with his left hand and shuts it.)

Hey, Jeff!

JEFF

(Doesn't respond, but looks up at Frank.[41])

FRANK

Heard you finally passed the Green level.

JEFF

Yeah? Where'd you hear that?

FRANK

Around.

(Shrugs)

Know what I think?

JEFF

Not much of anything?

(FRANK looks puzzled.)

What do you think?

FRANK

---

[41] Up his nose, actually. Not good.

43

I think that loser friend of yours can't count. And he lied. What'ya gunna do about that?

(JEFF opens his locker again and continues to pack his backpack. FRANK shuts the locker door again.)

You wouldn't let me pass Algebra. Why would I let you pass gym?

JEFF

No, I wouldn't let you cheat off my test in Algebra. You failed the class all on your own. You can't blame me for that.

FRANK

Can and will. I spent three days in after-school detention. Now you're cheating in gym. Can't allow it.

(Enter CAITLIN from stage left.)

CAITLIN

Can't allow what?

FRANK

Your boyfriend here is cheating in gym class.

CAITLIN

How do you cheat in gym? You either do it or you don't.

FRANK

Jeff here found a way. He had Mike lie for him.

CAITLIN

Jeff never lies.

FRANK

Oh really?

(FRANK crosses his arms, flexing his biceps and using his fists to push out the muscle to make them look bigger.)

Well, we'll see how he does next month at the challenge. I bet you won't get past Green again.

CAITLIN

He'll pass Blue!

FRANK

You're on!

JEFF & CAITLIN

(Speaking simultaneously)

What?

FRANK

It's a bet. Loser pays the winner $20.00.

CAITLIN

What level will you do?

FRANK

Purple.

CAITLIN

And you passed?

FRANK

I missed the last two pull-ups and was short by about 20 jump ropes.

CAITLIN

To make this fair, it will have to be equally challenging for you both. If Jeff did Green last week, then by next month he will do Blue. You did Purple today, so next month...GOLD.

FRANK

(smiling)

You're on.

(FRANK Turns and walks away.)

JEFF

What did you just do? I can't do Green.

CAITLIN

You just did Green.

(CAITLIN shrugs)

It's just a little more. And we have a whole month to train.

JEFF

(Speaking in a hissing whisper)

Except that I didn't do Green!

The Lie Entraps a Friend

"Friendship isn't a big thing—it's a million little things."
—Author Unknown

"You what?" Caitlin yelled. Thanks to Frank and the bet, we had missed the bus and were waiting for her mom to pick us up.

"It was Mike's idea. Or his mistake. My mistake. He didn't count right and told Mr. Pullup the wrong numbers and now I'm in trouble."

"I can't believe you lied," she said. "And I stood up for you!"

"Oh, I'm so dead," I groaned. "There's no way I can pass the circuit challenge and then Frank will know and Mike will be sent to the other school and I'll fail gym class, owe Frank twenty dollars, which I don't have, and there's no golf next year."

"Yeah. You're in a mess," Caitlin agreed.

"Thanks."

"And I made it worse. Accepting the challenge—I wish you had been honest with me at least."

"I'm sorry. But Frank was right there and if I said anything, he would have known. I just—I should have told the truth right away."

"But you didn't and I believed you, too. Now what are you going to do?" she asked.

47

"If I tell Mr. Pullup the truth, Mike loses. If I tell Frank the truth, both Mike and I lose. If I try to do the Challenge, I'll fail and lose twenty dollars. No matter what, there is no easy way out of this and Frank walks away looking good."

"Oh, but he's *so* not good," Caitlin fumed. "He's nothing but an overgrown, hairy bully who's just angry that you wouldn't let him cheat."

"Well, he'll win this."

"Not if you pass Blue," Caitlin said.

I laughed. "How likely is that?"

"If you train for it, it's totally possible." Her eyes took on her 'planning a big scheme' gleam. "Here's what we'll do: we'll train every day after school. Saturdays, too. I'll teach you how to jump rope. We'll run, do push-ups and everything. John Paul's weights are in the basement. We'll get you ready for Blue and Frank will lose."

"I don't know." It sounded good when she said it. It also sounded like a lot of work.

"You know what my brother would say," Caitlin smiled.

We both said, "Dig down deep." It was his motto.

"What do you have to lose?" she challenged. When I could think of nothing, she smiled. "We start today. Can you finish your homework by five and meet me at Anton Park?"

We met at the park behind our neighborhood at 5:15. Caitlin had a jump rope, a stop watch, a whistle, and a clip board.

"Seriously?" I asked.

"As your coach, there'll be none of that. Just do what I say."

Being quiet and going along with what my friends said was likely what put me in this mess in the first place. But

48

Mike was honest with his miscounting and Caitlin was as trapped as I was because I didn't tell her the truth. So, I stayed quiet and did everything Caitlin said. She had emailed John Paul and told him about my situation. He was able to reply quickly with a message of 'good luck' to me and a basic training schedule. Caitlin followed it to a 'T': running, pushups on park benches, sit-ups in the grass, an obstacle course through the playground, and more running. By the time I tried to jump rope, my legs were like jelly and I tangled the rope around my legs and fell.

"I think that's enough for today," Caitlin said, marking something on her clipboard. "Same time tomorrow."

I fell back into the grass trying not to puke. "Right. Remind me why we're doing this."

"Because Frank is a bully and deserves to be taught a lesson."

That was true, but in the back of my mind, I knew the lesson was mine. My screaming muscles agreed.

The next day, we did John Paul's basic training plan again. At first my arms and legs protested any movement, but after my second time running around the trail, I loosened up and actually felt strong.

"That was four seconds faster than yesterday!" Caitlin yelled. "Can you do two extra push-ups?"

I tried but it wasn't until Friday that I could. Caitlin set up a circuit training course just like at school.[42] I passed the Orange level, a milestone for me, but I couldn't celebrate with anyone but Caitlin because everyone else

---

[42] The wall jumps may have been a little lower, but I didn't care.

thought I had already passed Green. I had increased my speed around the track by seventeen seconds and I had, according to Caitlin's math, an overall improvement of twenty-two percent.

"Next Tuesday, you *will* pass Green," Caitlin encouraged. Then she blew her whistle and I ran the track in my best time ever.

Do I Really Belong to this Family?

"'Ohana means family—no one gets left behind, and no one is ever forgotten." –Chris Sanders and Dean DeBlois, Lilo & Stitch

Do I really belong to this family? I wonder if everyone asks that question? And if everyone does ask that question, why are members of a family so unique? My grandma tells me that when I'm mad I make the same face as my dad. And my dad tells me that I have the same walk as my mom. So there are some things that are unavoidably inherited: noses, hair, skin color. But other than those few things, my family's members are as different as a frog is from a horse.

Tonight at dinner I recorded the conversation on my iPod, just to prove to Alex, Mike and Jabari that no one in my family listens to each other. Here's the transcript:

MOM

Dinner's ready!

GEORGE

(Enters kitchen from basement)

Is it from a can? Or from the garden? Why can't we just order pizza?

DAD

(Closes laptop and carries it from the dining table to

the counter)

Smells wonderful, Mary Ellen. I love lasagna.

MOM

(Sighs as she carries a pot of soup)
It's minestrone. Amelia! Dinner!

JEFFERSON

(Already sitting at table, starving!)
She's still at practice.

GEORGE

Is there such a thing as pizza soup?

MOM

Amelia!
(Yelling up the stairs)
Come down now!

JEFFERSON

She's at practice.

DAD

I think the new website will stir up some new business.

GEORGE

Pepperoni soup. That could be good. Maybe I should go into the soup business. Soup, that's all we eat anymore.

MOM

Just what does that young lady think she's doing? We're all waiting.

DAD

Who?

MOM

Amelia. I've called her three times now.

JEFFERSON

(Says nothing. Why bother?)

GEORGE

I bet Amelia's as tired as I am of soup. She'd love pepperoni soup.

DAD

Go knock on her door, Jefferson.

JEFFERSON

She's not in her room.

MOM

Well, then run outside and call her in. I'll talk with her tonight about leaving the house without permission.

JEFFERSON

(Loses his patience, a trait he inherited from his father)
Mom! She's at *practice*!

DAD

(Ladling soup)
Don't talk to your mother that way.

MOM

(Dropping the napkins)
Oh! I was supposed to pick her up from practice! What time is it?

GEORGE

(Laughing)
Five forty-five.

MOM

(Grabbing the keys and running out the door)
I was supposed to pick her up at five!

At this point, Dad, George and I didn't know what to do. Dinner was hot and on the table, but without mom and Amelia, we weren't sure if we should go ahead and eat. So we waited. And the longer we waited, the better the minestrone soup smelled.

By the time mom and Amelia returned, we were ready to eat it cold. But first Amelia had to go wash her face because she'd been crying.

AMELIA

(Sobbing in the bathroom)

My own family forgot me! I can't believe it. No one remembered me for forty-five minutes. How *loved* do I feel right now?

(Said with thick sarcasm)

DAD

(Standing outside the bathroom with mom, who was also crying)

Honey, we love you. We're sorry.

GEORGE

(Under his breath)

Not as sorry as I am. I'm starving.

AMELIA

This wouldn't have happened if I had a cell phone. I could have called.

DAD

Why didn't you use someone else's cell phone?

AMELIA

Because I was the only one there!

DAD

There's no pay phone?

AMELIA

Oh, please, dad! It's not the '90's! Pay phones died along with cassette tapes!

MOM

Amelia, please come out, honey. We'll have dinner and figure out a way to avoid confusing the schedule again.

AMELIA

(Still sobbing)

It's because I'm a girl. If I was a boy, like George and Jefferson, you'd never forget me.

DAD

Now you know that's not true.

AMELIA

Have you ever forgotten them?

                         DAD
  Well, no.

                       AMELIA
  (Screaming sobs ensue.)

  And so on.
  The minestrone was heated again around ten o'clock
that night, but no one enjoyed it much because our
stomachs hurt so badly from hunger. Amelia was served
her soup in her room because she refused to eat with
people who forgot her.

Have I Broken the Code?

"Fitting in is a short-term strategy, standing out pays off in the long run." —Seth Godin

"What are you wearing to the dance?" my mom asked while I set the table.

"Clothes."

"Very funny. Does the dress code apply?"

"When doesn't it?" I asked.

"Do you need me to iron a shirt?"

"Mom, I'm just going to wear normal clothes. I don't care if my shirt is a little wrinkled." I also didn't want to show up all crisply ironed with my hair perfectly combed. That might indicate that I cared too much.

"Tie?" she asked hopefully.

"No tie. This is not a funeral. It's just a dance."

"Are you going to dance with anyone?"

"No one really dances at a dance, mom."

"Then why do they call it a dance?" she asked, mashing the potatoes with a little more fervor than necessary.

I didn't answer. I stared at her until she looked at me. "Mom. This conversation is finished. We talk about the same thing every time there's a dance."

She laughed and turned back to the potatoes. "I'm just trying to understand the youth of today," she said.

"Any luck?" I asked.

"Tons. So far I know that pants should be jeans, talking is slowly dying out of fashion as cell phone texting is the way to communicate, there is no dancing at a dance, and clothing should be casual, wrinkled, and just fit enough to pass the dress code but not by much, otherwise you're a nerd. How am I doing so far?"

"Pretty good," I agreed. "But I can't confirm any of it. That would be breaking the unspoken rule of keeping parents in the dark about social issues of today's teens."

Here are some terms my mom doesn't know. They would fall under the "School Dance Terminology" file—if I had a file of terms. I don't. I'm just saying that my mom would love to know these words because she wants to understand me better. I don't think knowing these would help her, but they might help you see what happens at school dances.

1. Standcing (v) - (pronounced "stand-sing") dancing as little as possible while standing and trying to look comfortable. This really comes down to swaying back and forth and moving your arms as if you are hammering.

2. Langdoned (v)- to be caught wearing lip gloss. The girls dress up and do something they think boys like to their hair. A few girls always sneak glittery lip gloss into the dance and put it on their lips behind a wall of friends. That's one of the things about girls I'll never understand; lipstick is not allowed, but they sneak it in and then wear it right on their face as if all the adult chaperones won't notice it. Mrs. Langdon always walks around with a box of tissues and a trash bag so the girls with extra shiny lips can wipe them off. To be "Langdoned" is to be caught with lipstick.

3. dweets (n) (pronounced like 'sweets but with a 'd'

instead of an 's') - applies to those who think they can dance but are really just embarrassing themselves.[43]

---

[43] It's important to know that Amber thinks everyone but the girls from her dance troop are dweets. They have been dancing together since preschool and do past routines to every song. Amber calls out a song title and they all rush to formation and begin.

Nightmare

"All emotion is involuntary when genuine." —*Mark Twain*

Unlike every other dance, I will never forget this one. Mike, Jabari and I were standing[44] around yelling at each other over the blaring music. We were watching Amber and her dance troop coordinate their routines and making demands of the DJ for music. The chips and punch were already gone and kids were awkwardly moving to and from the dance floor. Mrs. Langdon breezed by us with her box of tissues and girls ducked out of sight. It was all the normal dance stuff until Mr. and Mrs. Amore walked in.

I knew right away.

They were at the door talking with one of the teachers. Mrs. Amore held a tissue to her nose and Mr. Amore gestured frantically with his hands.

My stomach twisted.

The teacher gasped and put her hand to her mouth. She hugged Mrs. Amore, who nearly dissolved into a puddle of tears.

"No. No. No." I muttered. No one heard me, but Jabari saw the look on my face and turned to see Caitlin's parents walking toward her. She didn't see them right

---

[44] Not standcing!

59

away.

The world stopped.

I wanted the smile on Caitlin's face to last, but I knew it was all about to end. I was clear across the cafeteria. There was nothing I could do. And what could I do? My feet were stuck to the floor and my breath came in panicky spurts.

No. No. No!

Caitlin turned and saw her parents.

She knew.

They didn't have to tell her anything—their presence at the dance, Mrs. Amore's tears, the quivering of Mr. Amore's chin said it all.

Caitlin screamed. We could hear it above the music. "NO! NO!" she sobbed and backed away from her parents as if by denying the reality of their presence she could change the truth behind the reason they were there.

But truth is unchangeable.

Mr. Amore quickly gathered up Caitlin in his arms and they left.

"No." My mind was numb. My face felt hot. The music blared, but I only heard the echoing of Caitlin's cry. One of the parents ran to the DJ and had him turn off the music.

"Why did they turn it off?" Amber stopped dancing.

I grabbed her phone and called my dad.

"Hello?" my dad's voice floated out of the phone.

"John Paul's dead." The words were awful tasting in my mouth, bile and sour. "John Paul's dead!"

"I know, buddy," my dad said. "I'm on my way. I'll be right there!"

Who Will Eat the Cookies?

"I feel an army in my fist." —*Friedrich Schiller,* The Robbers

Amber snatched her phone back. "Honestly, Jeff. You are one ISB."

"What?" I yelled. "Speak English! I don't have time to translate your stupid lingo!"

She rolled her eyes. "One insanely strange boy." She walked away, texting to someone across the room.

I wanted to hit Amber. I've never wanted to hit a girl before, unless you count my sister. But I couldn't move. I just stood staring at her. How could she be so stupid? Didn't she just see what happened? She hadn't. Not until she reached her friends and hit 'Send' on her phone did she ask where Caitlin was.

I charged at her, intending on ripping that sparkling pink phone from her sparking pink fingers and smashing it to glittery bits on the floor. Jabari, who has completed the purple level in circuit and is much faster than me, caught up with me and pushed me outside just as my dad pulled up.

Dad's eyes were red and I immediately forgot about Amber and her phone. Jabari said something to my dad. I don't remember the rest. Thinking back, everything stopped for me. Maybe I even stopped breathing because I had a horrible pain in my chest and gut. We were home, all of us, crying in the family room. Dad didn't have much information, just that John Paul's squad was attacked.

"Tomorrow is going to be a long day," Dad said. "Get some sleep."

And then I was in bed. I don't think I even brushed my teeth.

I couldn't sleep. My best friend was hurting and I couldn't help her. I was hurting and couldn't help myself. All I thought about were all the ways I could pound on Amber and her cell phone and how impossible it was to think that John Paul was gone. He was alive when we baked the cookies for him and now he wasn't.

Who would eat those cookies?

Who would send Caitlin letters in the mail?

John Paul was dead.

Collecting John Paul

"As none can see the wind but in its effects on the trees, neither can we see the emotions but in their effects on the face and body."
—Terri Guillemets

The funeral wasn't scheduled until the next Saturday to give family and relatives from out of town time to fly or drive in, which meant that Caitlin would miss a full week of school. I don't normally see Caitlin much during the school day, but we have the same lunch period and we at least talk while we are in the lunch line, then she sits with her friends and I with mine. It was on the bus ride home that I missed her the most. I gathered the mail and checked the Amore's box, but it had already been picked up. Now I had no excuse to go to her house.

I finished my homework then went to the park to train. Maybe she would meet me there.

After stretching and doing a few exercises near the path to our houses, I decided to start without her. Caitlin wasn't coming. It looked like I would have to train for the circuit challenge alone.

And that made me mad—mad that Mike covered up his mistake with a lie, resentment toward Caitlin because she had made the bet with Frank and now wasn't here with her clipboard and stopwatch; and disappointed in myself that I had gone along with all the lies and plans. Irritation fueled my run. I was charging through the trail, crunching gravel and rocks with a vengeance, certain that if Caitlin was here with the stopwatch, this would have been my fastest run ever.

I trained faithfully all week from five until six thirty. I didn't want to let Caitlin down by not following through with John Paul's basic training. Maybe I was doing it for him. Maybe he would pull some heavenly strings and help me pass the Blue level. Maybe I'm just a dreamer.

By Thursday, the morning news crew at school had pieced together a memorial report on John Paul Amore. It included pictures from the Junior and Senior High yearbook archive, put to music. As the pictures slid across the screen, I couldn't look. John Paul was a goof ball in school. He was smiling and happy and completely unaware in these pictures that he only had a few more years to live.

There was a moment of silence after that report.

That silence lasted all day for me.

On Friday, I decided to save my homework for Sunday and was at the park by three-thirty. Caitlin was sitting on a swing. Her face was streaked with dirt. I couldn't imagine what her day had been like and why she was dressed in her Sunday best but splattered with mud. For just a moment, I almost turned around and went home, but she saw me.

"Hi," I said, stupidly.

She nodded, but didn't say anything.

I asked one more question. "Did you fall?"

She shook her head.

Instead of talking or training or doing homework or baking cookies for John Paul, we sat on the swings and said nothing. From the path, Mrs. Amore called that Caitlin needed to come home for dinner. She wasn't wearing an apron, which meant that she had probably heated one of the dozen casseroles that the neighbors had poured on them. Caitlin quietly walked toward home.

"See you tomorrow," I called out.

She didn't say anything. I would see her tomorrow at the funeral. Then it hit me. I knew where she had been and why she was dressed up. Mom told me that sometime this week they would drive to Virginia to collect John Paul.

Collect him.

Not welcome him home with homemade banners and hugs and a party, but collect him. They had watched as his American-flag draped coffin was marched off a plane. Mom said there was a quiet ceremony then the drive home behind a hearse. That explained Caitlin's clothes, but why was she covered with mud? Where had she been?

After Caitlin left, I went home too. Everything seemed trivial. I would give anything—I mean anything—to have John Paul be alive. I'd give up the hopes of ever having a cell phone just to have him walk into Caitlin's room and tell her a story. I'd wear old, worn-out clothes for the rest of my life if somehow John Paul's letters would continue. I would sit in a booster seat in the car and at restaurants and at school for the rest of my life if it meant that John Paul would once again sit across from Caitlin at dinner.

I used to think I didn't have much: second-hand clothes, parents who were stressed out about money all the time, no cable TV, no cell phone, no wii or Xbox. Caitlin has all that, but now it seems like she has nothing. I have a family who has not been touched by death. Caitlin's family? How will this affect them? Will Mr. and Mrs. Amore stay married? I've seen in movies that sometimes couples who lose a child get divorced. I can't imagine Caitlin's family being torn to pieces like that, but John Paul is gone, and I'm having trouble imagining that, too.

He was supposed to come home in two months. Mrs. Amore was planning on doing a big yard party with barbecue and corn on the cob and music and all his friends and family. She was going to order a cake from the bakery and drape streamers neatly around the fence and celebrate the safe return of her son with perfectly cut sandwiches served on red, white, and blue plates with matching cups and napkins.

Did John Paul know that he wouldn't be coming home? Was he afraid when it happened? Were his last thoughts about Caitlin? Were other soldiers killed too? Did he save anyone?

His death was mentioned in the news, but it didn't say anything about him or the situation or his family. No one watching that news cast would know the real tragedy of his death. People probably just continued eating their supper when they heard the report and didn't even take a moment to say a prayer for his family. No one watching the news would understand how ripped up his family was and how much support and prayer they needed. At the end of the segment mentioning John Paul's death, the news reporter slapped on a smile and moved onto the next report, a new study that suggests people who play video games, particularly the violent ones that have realistic graphics and a first-person point-of-view, have a greater tendency to act out violently in real-life situations.

Would it have been so awful for the newscaster to ask everyone watching to take one minute of silence to commemorate the fallen heroes of our Nation?

If the Good Really Do Die Young, What's My Inspiration to Be Good?

"I used to believe in forever, but forever is too good to be true."
—A.A. Milne, Winnie-the-Pooh

I've only been to one funeral before; my great-uncle Fred died of extreme old age. If there was a way for a body to slowly wear out over one-hundred three years, his did it. The walls of the funeral were lined with poster boards with photo collages. There was even a big screen T.V. that had a slide show of pictures set to the song, "I Will Remember You". The pictures of Great-Uncle Fred ranged from black & white and stoic faces to yellowing memories of the 50's and 60's to newly printed digital shots. He was young, straight and crisply dressed in some, or covered with dirt while holding a shovel or a pick in others. As I walked along the wall, he aged slowly. His ears got bigger while all his kids made him look shorter.

My brother and I made a game of trying to figure out who was who from the older pictures. All of Great-Uncle Fred's kids are much older than my parents, so they were the hardest to identify. We concluded that men don't age as well as women, but women tend to end up bigger.[45]

I didn't see Great-Uncle Fred outside of the annual family Christmas party. Our conversations were limited to: Hello. Whose kid are you? Oh, really? I didn't know she had children. What? You're the youngest?

Children and grandchildren, distant relatives and friends had packed the room, the hallway and even the sidewalk outside. Tears dripped from every eye at some point, but I heard many times, "What a good, long life he lived."

John Paul's funeral was different. He had only lived for twenty-one years. No photographs had faded to yellow. The people in the pictures—John Paul's friends and family—hadn't aged much at all. There was no who's-who game, not that I felt like playing anyway.

I knew John Paul. Knew him well. He lived next door. He was Caitlin's brother, the best tire swing pusher and freeze-tag player ever born.

It took a while to find Caitlin; she stood quietly next to her grandmother, while her parents stood like sentinels by the closed casket. Questions pounded on my brain and I had to bite my cheek to keep from asking them: Was John Paul really in that coffin? Why was it closed? Were they certain it was John Paul? Could they have made a mistake?

Caitlin saw me and I waved. She beckoned me over. I was suddenly nervous. What should I say? What if I said something wrong? What if I made her cry? Would she act differently?

I shook those thoughts out as soon as they came. This was Caitlin. My friend. Of course she would cry. Of

---

[45]My sister both liked and hated this conclusion. And, of course, George teased her that while she might end up with fewer wrinkles, she'd be too fat to care.

course she's going to act differently.

"Hi." I felt stupid.

"Hi."

I stood next to her, feeling awkward and very out of place. "Should I leave you be?" I asked. "I don't want to get in the way."

Caitlin's eyes filled with tears. "Stay." She grabbed my hand and squeezed.

I nodded.

Then I blushed.

We were holding hands.

I've known Caitlin forever, but we've never held hands. We've played together the way kids do every summer, all summer, and at every recess during grade school. We've held hands for Red Rover, but this was different. Holding her hand now wasn't romantic or anything dumb like my sister talks about with her friends. It was necessary.

I purposely didn't make eye contact with my brother. I knew he wanted to tease me for holding a girl's hand. My mom smiled at me and dad patted my shoulder—it was a "you're a good friend to her" pat and I felt proud.

It seemed like hundreds of people[46] walked by, talking to Caitlin and her grandmother, but Caitlin said very little. She gripped my hand as if she had fallen off a cliff and I was keeping her from plummeting to the rocky bottom. When I looked at Caitlin's hand, it was white from the effort. It was also grimy. Her fingernails were brown with dirt and a little scratched. I could see grass stains on her

---

[46] Including many of the teachers from school, which was odd. They were all red-eyed and normal. They were people grieving a terrible loss. It changed the way I saw them all. They didn't view the students as factory productions, after all, teaching them what they can and passing them to the next level.

knees and a smudge of dirt on her jaw. What had she been doing? Why would she come to her brother's funeral all grubby? Was she so sad that she couldn't shower? This is the girl who showers after playing in the sprinklers and washes her hands after washing the dishes.

At some point, the crowd left the funeral home and walked down the street to the church. The sidewalk was lined with kids from school, and a few police cars had blocked traffic so we could just walk the two blocks in the street behind the hearse. Soldiers dressed in all kinds of military uniforms stood along the road too, all saluting John Paul.

Caitlin's family is Catholic. The priest wore a white robe and the altar servers were kids from school. The priest used incense and filled the entire church with a smoky sadness, smelling of comfort, of something important, and strong enough to make my eyes water. He talked about life and death and how we can't understand God's timing, but we must trust it. I hoped he wouldn't say that something good comes from every situation, and he didn't. What good could happen from John Paul's death?

As I sat in that church, surrounded by all the people who knew and loved John Paul and dozens of statues, I began to wonder about heaven. A funeral Mass is a natural time to wonder about it, I guess. I'd never gone to church regularly like the Amores do, but sitting there, looking through the haze of incense smoke at the statues, I realized that heaven was probably a real place. Here was a whole church filled with reminders that heaven was real. And if heaven was real, it was likely that John Paul was there.

Maybe that was the something good. Heaven.

The priest talked about the next life, the resurrection,

the hope in Jesus that this life is not the end of everything. I liked what he said. If there is a next—something—then I wanted to have it. If John Paul had been an altar boy, had sat in these pews listening to the lessons of the Bible, if he really was in heaven, then I wanted that, too.

I wanted to ask Caitlin about it as I rode back to Caitlin's house with her and her grandmother, but it wasn't the right time. It was a quiet ride. Caitlin didn't hold my hand. She looked out the window and seemed farther away from me than Polaris.[47] My parents and a few other neighbors were already at her house, setting up a potluck dinner and cleaning the kitchen. We ate a little, but no one seemed very hungry. Talk was quiet as the adults planned breakfast for Caitlin's family the next morning.

As the evening stretched, the mood lightened a bit and neighbors began to share stories about John Paul. He had babysat almost all of their children. Parents would come home and find their living room furniture stripped of the cushions and used as bricks to build giant forts. Little by little, laughter replaced the stillness. I looked to where Caitlin was sitting to see if she was laughing, too.

She was gone.

I checked the kitchen. "Caitlin?"

"She's slipped out again," Mrs. Amore said as she brought her glass to the sink.

"Again?" my mother asked.

Mrs. Amore smiled sadly.[48] "She's not running away, as

---

[47] That's the North Star, just in case you haven't studied that in school yet.

[48] I know that sounds contradictory—to smile sadly—a true oxymoron if there ever was one, but that's the best description. She smiled because she knew how hard all this was on Caitlin—it was a

we first feared. She just goes for long walks. At least that's what she tells us."

"Through the mud," Caitlin's grandma joined in.

"Mom," Mrs. Amore sighed the way Amelia does when our mom pesters her.[49]

"Well," Caitlin's Grandma shrugged, "the poor little thing was filthy at her own brother's funeral. What will people think?"

I didn't hear Mrs. Amore's answer. I left in search of Caitlin. Her bedroom door was open, but I still knocked. "Caitlin?" Pushing the door open all the way, I closed my eyes, just in case, and stepped in. "Caitlin? Are you in here?"

She wasn't.

Her room had changed since last summer. There were new drawings and sketches taped to her walls. Many of her stuffed animals had been packed away, but Mr. Jangles, her favorite teddy bear, had the prime spot on the bed. Her desk was cluttered with half-started homework.

The top of her dresser was much like a mini-museum, a collection of valued treasures that held no monetary value but oozed a wealth of memories. A box covered with pictures of her and John Paul sat in the center. Many of the smaller items that had been on the dresser for years were gone. I peeked inside the box to confirm my suspicions; all of John Paul's letters were neatly tucked inside, organized by date.

My stomach felt empty. I missed him. And if I felt this way, how awful must Caitlin be feeling? Where was she,

---

knowing smile. It made her sad, too, to not know why Caitlin was leaving the house unannounced. While her mouth smiled, her eyes were teary. "Such is the emotion of a mother with a broken heart and an inconsolable daughter," my mom said later.

[49] Apparently parents and children never outgrow this.

anyway?

The dress she had worn earlier lay forgotten on the floor and the window had been propped open with the screen. I caught a glimpse of the reflective tape on her backpack as she ducked under the fence.

I couldn't imagine why she had left through the window or why she had left at all. And why hadn't she told me she was leaving?

Hesitating, I looked back out her bedroom door to the living room. The adults could talk for hours—or they could call it a night in five minutes and then come looking for us. Either way I wasn't going to let Caitlin sneak off by herself.

She had a flashlight and a bright backpack which made it easy to follow. She was heading to Anton Park.

But it was dark and Anton Park closes at dusk. What *was* she doing? Should I watch from behind trees and park benches? Be a spy and discover the mystery of the grubby girl at the funeral?

No. Caitlin was my friend. She was obviously suffering a severe mental breakdown. Why else would she go to a park at night?

"Caitlin!" I called out running to catch up. She turned, holding up a small shovel as if she intended to bludgeon my head. "It's me." I held up my hands, surrendering.

She sighed and lowered the shovel. "Jeff! You scared me half to--"

Silence.

Half to death. That's what she was going to say. Death was too close right now.

"What are you doing?" she asked.

"Me?" I acted casual. "Oh, you know, just taking a stroll through the park at night, following a girl with a shovel. What are *you* doing?"

73

Turning, she walked farther into the park. "I have to find it."

I followed. "What?"

She was crying again. "A time capsule."

That explained nothing. Stepping in front of her so she had to stop, I crossed my arms. "Tell me."

Her eyes were bright red and her nose was dripping. She looked so sad. I didn't know what to do, so I just waited. "Before John Paul left for the war, he and I made a time capsule. We put important things in it, but we didn't tell each other what they were. We were going to dig it up when he came home and see what had been so important to us before."

That made sense. "Where is it?"

"I don't remember."

"You weren't with him when he buried it?"

"I was." She wiped her eyes. "I didn't think I would have to dig it up alone."

The park's wooded section shaded a paved path for three-quarters of a mile. There could easily be a thousand trees in there. How would we ever find one little box? Visions of Caitlin and I digging as wrinkly senior citizens popped into my head.[50] I also imagined how happy she would be when we found it.

"You aren't alone."

---

[50] Me wrinkly with big ears and her fat and wearing a house dress.

Is That Okay?

"Friendship...is born at the moment when one man says to another 'What! You too? I thought that no one but myself...'" —
C.S. Lewis

I knew she would be coming back to school today. Her mom told my mom, and my mom told me to be extra nice to her. As if I needed a reminder to do that.

But all the kids at school became walking idiots. Her return was big news and all the girls whispered about it too loudly and Caitlin heard them. Then some girls talked about Caitlin's brother again and how he died (or how they think he died) and Caitlin heard that, too. At lunch, she sat with her friends, but none of them spoke to her and just talked about things that happened while she was gone, so she had nothing to contribute.

Halfway through lunch, she looked at my lunch table and I smiled.

She smiled back.

Then to my surprise she picked up her lunch tray and started walking toward my lunch table.

"Hi."

"Are you going to sit with us?" I tried to make it sound like an invitation, but I was really just shocked that she would leave her friends. And judging from the look of horror on her friends' faces, they were, too.

"Is that ok?"

"Sure!" We all said together, sounding a little too eager and like complete morons. She giggled and sat down with us.

"How is your first day back?" Jabari asked. I cringed. Are you supposed to ask someone who just lost a brother in the war how they are?

"Terrible." She poked her lunch with her fork. "Everyone seems to have developed a fear of me. All my friends are treating me like I'm going to explode."

"Well, sure," Jabari said. "They don't know what to say and so they feel nervous."

"You think that's it?" Caitlin asked.

"Yeah," Jabari said. "At my old school, when my mom died, that's what it was like for me."

We all stared at Jabari. I knew his mom was dead, but I never really thought about what it had been like for him. "I'm sorry," Caitlin said. "I didn't know."

Jabari shrugged. "It was five years ago. I think it's easier when you're younger. You don't really understand it all. People will forget about it after a while."

She took a bite of her lunch. "I guess I just expected everyone to treat me like they always did. I was hoping that I could come here and find it just like it was. You know normal. But even Mrs. Swen skipped current events today and I think it was because of me."

"It probably was," Mike said, "but it was my turn, so I'm glad you came back today."

Caitlin chuckled.

"The funeral was nice," Jabari said. "I really was glad that so many soldiers were there. Made it really special."[51]

---

[51] There he goes again! Just saying whatever comes to mind. How can he just talk about something so sad? I wish I was brave like that.

76

Caitlin nodded. "I didn't know they would do that. I don't think any of those soldiers knew my brother, so it was really nice of them to be there."

"There's a strong sense of brotherhood in the service," Jabari said. "My dad was in the Navy. He's been to tons of funerals."

"Doesn't it make him sad to do that?" Caitlin asked. "I mean, to be around so much sadness all the time. To see so many soldiers' families cry?"

"I think it used to. But he told me once that death comes for everyone. It's up to those who are left behind to stick together. Being at the funerals is his way of honoring those soldiers. Being there for the family, even if it's only for one day, shows respect and honor."

A Letter From Beyond

"Feelings are much like waves, we can't stop them from coming, but we can choose which ones to surf." —Jonatan Mårtensson

"Being the subject of gossip is exhausting." Caitlin dragged herself off the bus and hoisted her backpack.

"What do you mean?"

"Kids I've never met asked me today exactly how John Paul died. My friends ignored me. Teachers piled on the homework, but told me I didn't have to do it. People either feel sorry for me or are afraid of me."

I knew that. I was one of them. We stopped at the mailboxes. Caitlin glanced over to Amber, who was busy on her phone, and whispered, "Amber talked about John Paul as if she knew him. She's never even been to my house."

I didn't know what to say. She was right about everything. I almost said, "Tomorrow will be better," but I didn't because it probably wouldn't be. It might be months before it's better.

Suddenly, Caitlin gasped, dropped the mail and her backpack, and ran toward her house.

Without stopping to help me as I picked it all up, Amber strolled by. "What was that about?"

My hands shook as I reached for the mail. One envelope had an American flag and a hand written address on the front; on the back was a teddy bear sticker.

"It's a letter from John Paul."

Amber looked at the envelope over my shoulder. "I thought he was dead. How could he send her mail? Oh!" she gasped and covered her mouth, her eyes growing bigger than the screen on her phone. "Is this a letter from beyond?"

My mouth opened and out poured the punchiest words I could think of. I wanted to hurt Amber, but I knew I couldn't touch her so I made every word cut like broken glass. [52] Amber told her mom what I said, and her mom called my mom. I'm forbidden to even think of those words again, so I'll edit the content and replace it with art terminology.

"Amber, you are the *ink blot* in the whole *hue* school. If you would take five *paintbrush* minutes and think about the people who are right in front of your *turpentine* face you might be considered a *color wheel* person. But you're not! You're a selfish, conceited brat with less heart than the *blankest canvas*. I hope you drop your cell phone in a *Picasso* toilet!"

I carried Caitlin's backpack and mail to her house. Mrs. Amore had been crying too but said she was very grateful that I had brought everything home for Caitlin. I handed her the letter. Her hands shook.

"Can I see Caitlin?" I asked.

Mrs. Amore looked at the kitchen. The counters were covered with dishes piled upon more dishes. Flowers and plants from the funeral covered the dining room table and most of the floors. "Maybe she'll talk to you. She's in her room."

---

[52] OK, physically I *could* have touched her—really hurt her. But I knew I *shouldn't*.

Caitlin was lying on her bed holding Mr. Jangles. She wasn't crying, just lying perfectly still.

"I'm sorry," I said. It was all I could think of to say, but it seemed inadequate. I wasn't sorry for something I had done, but for not knowing what to do.

"It scared me," she whispered.

I sat down at her desk and she looked at me. "I understand," I said.

"Do you?" Her voice was crazy with sarcasm. I knew she just wanted to yell at someone, to be angry and let all her sadness out.

"I think so. You are hurting way in here," I pointed to my stomach, "but nothing helps. Stupid people keep telling you that it will get easier with time, but that just makes you hurt more. Everywhere you look you see things that make you think of John Paul. All you want is to wake up and have all this be a dream. But you can't because it's not and that hurts more. So you just want to sleep because when you're asleep it hurts less. But those stupid people are telling you to get on with living, that it will somehow get better if you stop thinking about the past. Friends at school are trying to share the hurt with you, except they didn't know him. They pretend to be sad for your sake, but they don't understand what it means to be this sad.

"The past is all you want. And it won't come back no matter how much you bargain with God. And that hurts the most; to feel that God isn't hearing you."

Caitlin struggled to hold back her tears. She had caged her emotions and they were clawing at her to get out. I knelt by her bed. "Caitlin, it's just me. You can cry. It's OK. I won't tell anybody."

She covered her face with her hands. Her muffled voice was stretched. "It will make me weak. John Paul was so strong, so brave. I don't want to disappoint him."

I pulled her hand away from her face and held it tight.

"I miss him," she sobbed. "I'll never see my brother again. He won't ever celebrate another birthday. He won't get the present I bought him for Christmas. He won't come home ever again! He won't be here. I just want him back. It's not fair! He was so good. So good! Everybody says so. Why him?"

Caitlin cried and cried. I cried too, mostly because she was so sad and it made me hurt to see her that way. I could hear Mrs. Amore standing just outside the room sniffing and trying to be quiet. I stayed where I was, holding Caitlin's hand. There was nothing for me to say. No words would make her feel better, and anything I might say would be stupid attempts to deny her from feeling what she was supposed to feel. It occurred to me as she cried that this was exactly what she needed— permission to cry and the opportunity to say everything she felt out loud.

Anger.

Pain.

Sadness.

Fear.

Loneliness.

All those horrible feelings were festering away inside her. She didn't want to hear that it would all be better someday, she needed to feel safe today; safe in her sadness, safe in knowing that sadness wasn't weakness.

What Now?

"Be nimble. Be quick. Make that obstacle a candlestick."
—Jessica Schaub

I don't know if the next day was easier for Caitlin. She didn't talk about it and I didn't ask. After school we fell into our old patterns. We met at the park after we had finished our homework, except now we weren't training for the Circuit Challenge. We were hunting for buried treasure. We had no map of where John Paul had buried the box, and Caitlin's memory only gave us a section of the park where she remembered being when he'd buried it. She said the tree was tall and near a park bench with a large branch that stuck straight out and had no leaves.

"That doesn't help very much," I said, surveying the parks wooded section. "You've just described almost half the trees."

"I drew it." She handed me a folded piece of paper with a drawing of a tree. We spent the next two days examining every tree from every angle. We couldn't find a match.

"Let's look through the park again," I suggested, "but this time, look for other things that would be indicators."

"Like what?"

"Like this knot you drew above this branch here. Maybe that's what we need to look for."

"Not the straight branch?"

"I think maybe that has fallen off and that's why we can't find the tree."

Caitlin looked around the park. "Great."

I checked my watch. "It's after 7:00. We should get home."

Reluctantly, Caitlin left the park. She never said anything, but I could see that the search was wearing on her. Between school, catching up with all the work she missed, and searching for the tree, she wasn't sleeping well. We didn't search for the tree over the weekend; our parents kept us all busy with chores on Saturday and then we spent Sunday afternoon on homework. Caitlin's mom insisted she stay home and work to catch up, so it was Monday after school before we were able to get back to the park.

And when we stepped onto the trail, our hearts stopped.

A wide section of chain-link fencing had been taken down and the gap closed with yellow construction tape. A large backhoe and several trucks were parked next to the playground. A truck with a lift was parked right on the trail with the lift high in the trees. As we watched open mouthed, a limb the size of a car fell with a crack and woosh.

"What—?" Caitlin gasped.

"Hey! You kids get back!" A man wearing a yellow hard hat and an orange vest walked toward us. "Can't you see that sign?"

We hadn't seen it, to tell the truth. It was large and orange and very untimely:

**Anton Park Closed for
construction of basketball courts
Reopens on May 30th**

"What?" Caitlin yelled. "You can't just close the park! It's public property!"

The man raised his eyebrows. "Look kid, the neighborhood voted in these improvements. We can't work on taking down the trees and pouring cement for the court with kids all over the place. It will only be closed for a few weeks."

Caitlin stared at the mess the men were making. "What do we do now?"

"Find another park," the man said. "And stay out of here until we're done. It's dangerous with all this equipment here."

We walked away, but only so far as the other side of the fence where we watched four trees come down. "We'll have to come back after dark," Caitlin decided.

"The park is closed at dark," I said. "It's even closed during the day."

Caitlin pointed to a new sign next to the sidewalk. It had a new map of the park with the pending improvements. "Do you know what kinds of improvements they're making? They are cutting down that section of trees," she pointed to where we had been digging for the time capsule. "If they pave it, I will never find the box."

"Oh."

"I'm coming out here tonight," she said. "Will you help me?"

"Okay."

It was harder than I thought to sneak out of the house at night. I could have asked George for help, but I didn't trust him to keep it a secret. After dinner, I gathered together a flashlight and a small shovel into my backpack.

Dad asked why I needed a flashlight. I didn't want to lie—I've had enough bad luck with that, so I told him Caitlin needed it but that I didn't know why. Dad didn't question it and I went back to my room. At ten thirty, I snuck into the kitchen and slipped out the back door. Caitlin was already waiting for me at the park.

Looking up at trees in the dark with only the help of a flashlight proved to be slow going. The light was only strong enough to illuminate the lower parts of the trees, and only a small section at a time. It was after one in the morning when we finally found a knot in a tree that looked like her drawing. "I think that's it."

Caitlin shone her light on the knot. "Yeah. Maybe."

"Well it's the closest match so far."

She walked up to the tree and put her hand on the trunk. "It's dead. Look right there." She pointed with her flashlight to a section of the tree that had been torn away from the trunk. "I bet there used to be a long, straight branch there."

"Jackpot!" I cried.

She was smiling, the first smile in weeks. "Let's start digging."

And dig we did. But digging in the dark added a layer of creepiness. The flashlight didn't give much light. The shovel kept hitting the roots of the tree. Stones blocked our progress. Insects can apparently see perfectly in the dark and found their ways up our arms and pant legs. We dug for an hour that first night before the flashlight gave out. We walked home in the dark, promising each other that we would meet again the following night at midnight.

Tuesday and Wednesday night, we dug until two in the morning with no success.

"Are you sure this is the right tree?" I asked Caitlin as we walked home early Thursday morning.

85

"No. But it's the best match. Let's dig one more night."

"Fine, but not tomorrow night. I'm exhausted. I almost fell asleep in science class today."

"Friday night then," Caitlin reluctantly agreed. "It looks like the workmen are still taking down trees. I don't think they will start on paving the court until next week. They unloaded the gravel today, so they'll have to spread that before they pave."

I laughed. "Since when are you an expert on pavement procedures?"

"Google. I wanted a better idea of our time line for digging."

I went to bed early Thursday night. My mother thought I was coming down with a cold, so she let me sleep in Friday morning and drove me to school so I could sleep an extra thirty minutes. "Can we give Caitlin a ride too?" I asked.

"Yep. I called her mom last night. She agreed that Caitlin could use the extra sleep. I don't think she's sleeping that well. I hope she isn't catching your cold."

I didn't tell her that my 'cold' was from a complete lack of sleep because I had been sneaking out of the house at night to help Caitlin dig around the base of a tree. Even as I thought that, it sounded strange. Sneaking out of the house? That's so George. And he's been grounded for months at a time for it. I swallowed my cereal and felt sick. It's one thing to help a friend; it's another to deceive my parents. Why do they go together so often?

Will I be Rewarded for Being a Good Friend, or Punished for Breaking the Rules?

"Where you treasure is, there also your heart will be."
—Matthew 6:21

"Over there, by the trail," a woman's voice drifted over the ground.

We clicked off our flashlights and froze. My heart beat so loudly I couldn't hear anything. Caitlin leaned close to me. "I think someone saw us."

"We should go," I whispered back. "Come on."

"Jeff, we finally found the tree. Let's wait." She grabbed my arm and pulled me down into the hole we had dug.

The voices were closer. "And you saw flashlights, ma'am?"

Ma'am?

"Yes, Officer. Just over there."

Even in the dark I could see Caitlin's face go pale. "Police!" I whispered. "Come on!"

We dashed out from the tree and ran down the trail toward our houses. Once through the gate by the sidewalk, we dove behind the wall of cedar trees and lay flat on the ground. Our breathing seemed as loud as a siren indicating where we were, but the police officer never came near us. We didn't hear anymore talking and assumed after ten minutes we were safe.

"Oh my gosh, my heart is still pounding," Caitlin said, sitting up.

"Nothing compared to mine," Mr. Amore's voice spoke from behind us. "Stand up, both of you."

We did as told and stepped onto the sidewalk to face four angry parents and one smiling police man. "Well," the police officer said, "that mystery is solved."

My dad shook hands with him and thanked him for his help. Then we marched back to Caitlin's house where we were put on trial and sentenced.

"The middle of the night?" Mr. Amore was trying really hard to not yell. "Do you have any idea how afraid we were? Why are you doing this, Caitlin? Haven't we suffered enough already? Do we really need to add more stress to our lives?"

Caitlin couldn't speak. Tears slipped down her cheeks and she sat there not saying anything.

"Jeff?" my dad spoke up, "can you tell us what's going on?"

"Yes sir." And I did. I told them all about the time capsule and that John Paul had buried it but Caitlin couldn't remember where. I told them about the construction crew that was going to pave the trail and possibly cover the time capsule forever and then Caitlin would never see the box again and how that just wasn't fair because she had already lost so much.

When I was finished, the adults just stared at us.

"I see." Mr. Amore finally managed. "I'll call the construction company in the morning and see if we can suspend their work for a while. Then we'll all go to the park and look for the box." Caitlin ran to her father and hugged him. And cried. There was lots of crying. Caitlin's sentence was that she had to go to bed right away[53] and never scare her parents like that again.

My sentencing was much different. I had to go to bed too, but they woke me early the next morning and I had to do all the Saturday morning chores by myself. Mom gave Amelia and George money to go see a movie and I stayed home sweeping, mopping, vacuuming and scrubbing toilets. "We are doing this because you weren't honest with us," my dad said. "I know you were helping Caitlin, and we think that is very honorable, but you lied to us. That is not honorable."

"So I'm being punished for being a good friend, but not telling you about it?"

My parents exchanged a look. Dad nodded. "Yeah. That pretty much sums it up."

Just as I was finishing the downstairs bathroom, Caitlin ran into the house, yelling. "Jeff! They're up there now. Dad couldn't stop them. They're cutting down my tree!"

I dropped the dust cloth and ran with Caitlin to the park. My dad followed. We stood along the fence watching the crew efficiently cut down the tree. Starting at the top they removed one dead limb after another. They fell heavily to the earth, sending vibrations all the way through the ground to where we stood. My dad put his arm around Caitlin as she cried; all her hopes of finding the time capsule were gone.

"Maybe they'll find it when they dig up the tree," I said, hoping my suggestion would manifest itself into reality.

"No. They just chip the trunk into a pile of sawdust,

---

[53] It was, after all, almost 2:30 AM.

spread it around and go over it with the pavement," my dad said, destroying all hopes.

Then there was nothing to do but watch the park's trees be annihilated for a basketball court. Thoughts of saving the day danced around in my imagination. Maybe I could sabotage the equipment, giving us time to dig under the tree. Maybe I could chain myself to the tree and stop the work. Maybe I could—and then I would be arrested. I'd be the only kid in school with a criminal record. And they don't let criminals play golf in high school.

Come on, God, I prayed. *Do something! Caitlin has lost everything. Give her this. Give her this last treasure from John Paul.*

And God acted. Right there and then, God showed up.

It happened in a way that I didn't expect, because do we ever really expect God to act that quickly on a prayer?

As the workmen drove the lift toward the tree to take down its top limbs, the truck lurched forward, smashing into the tree. A *crack* as loud as a gunshot resounded through the park as the wood and earth gave under all the pressure. Men were yelling at the driver to back up, but he seemed unable to make the truck do anything. The tree swayed as the ground around the base of the trunk lifted, shooting dirt and stones up into the air.

Mrs. Amore and my mom came running toward the park.

"Back it up!" a rotund workman shouted at the driver.

"*Bleeping*[54] truck won't do a *bleeping* thing!" the driver yelled back.

"Shift it down! Shift it down!"

That seemed to do it and the truck lurched backwards.

---

[54] Again, I've taken the liberty of editing the language so as to make this appropriate reading material for kids our age.

And then Caitlin saw it. As the tree fell, bringing up its roots and everything, she saw the box. Jumping the fence, she ran toward the falling tree.

"Caitlin!" my dad yelled, following her over the fence. "Caitlin! Stop!"

I watched as Caitlin ran toward the falling tree, which fell slowly, ripping up more and more ground. The roots snapped, spraying dirt everywhere. Caitlin was close to the tree now and she seemed to have realized that it wasn't safe to get any closer until it had fallen all the way. My dad saw a greater danger. A squeaking rub of wood against wood alerted us all to a collision happening about twenty feet up. A large limb on the falling tree snagged on an oak, and stopped the descent for a moment.

"She's gonna snap!" a workmen yelled at my dad. "Get her—"

SNAP! CRACK! WHOOSH!

The limb snapped off and was flung in the opposite direction of the tree falling. I couldn't see what happened, but I saw the limb heading straight for Caitlin. My dad grabbed her and kept running for a few more steps then they both fell to the ground.

Mrs. Amore screamed, and my mother jumped the fence and ran toward them. The rest of us scrambled around to the gate and followed. The limb was just a few feet away from my dad and Caitlin, who had fallen into the hole made when the tree's roots had lifted out of the ground.

"Caitlin!" Mrs. Amore yelled. "Are you hurt?"

We all looked into the hole and saw my dad and Caitlin at the bottom, covered with dirt.

"Caitlin!" she yelled again.

"I'm fine."

"Jeff?" my mom's voice quavered.

"Nothing broken, dear."

"Caitlin, what are you doing?" Mrs. Amore climbed down into the hole. "You nearly got yourself and Mr. Stanhope killed."

Caitlin didn't answer. She pulled the box her brother had buried all those months ago from among the tangle of exposed roots.

A little battered, covered with thick patches of mud and crawling with centipedes and spiders, was John Paul and Caitlin's time capsule.

Only we understood the importance of the moment. The workmen, however, were furious. "Would all you crazy folks get out of that hole? What is going on?"

"I'm very sorry," my mother turned to the red-faced man and explained everything that had happened. As she told them about the time capsule and John Paul's death, the work man finally softened the angry creases on his forehead. He removed his yellow hard hat.

"Come on, folks. I have bolt cutters in my truck. I can snap that lock off for you."

Caitlin clung to the box, her face smeared with grime. "I know the combination." She knelt right there at the base of the fallen oak. Her hands shook as she spun the dial and opened the box.

Mrs. Amore gasped. On top was a picture of John Paul in his combat fatigues, smiling as if nothing was wrong in the world. There were an envelope, a small box and a small stuffed teddy bear with a yellow ribbon around his neck. Caitlin set the picture of John Paul on the inside of the lid and took out the envelope. In his neat handwriting, John Paul gave Caitlin another great gift: one more letter.

Hey Kit-Kat!

This is a tough letter to write. I'm not sure where I'll be when you read it— maybe you are old and gray and finally remembered that we planted this box in the park; or maybe things didn't go how we planned and I never came home from the war. Either way, I'm glad you found the box and are remembering me.

Just in case I'm not there, I pray that this box will bring you peace. I won't lie to you, I don't want to die and I'm a little afraid of death. But, as Grandpa always said, "It happens to everybody, so why worry?"

So I'm not going to worry about death. But I do worry about you. If I didn't come home, that means you are now an only child. Yes, you can have my room and everything in it. Give Jeff my baseball glove and all my trading cards. He always liked looking at them. But for you, I leave you everything else. There's some money under my bed: I think you should use it for college, but it's yours now, so do what you want with it.

Can I make a dying request? Is that too morbid? Well, here goes anyway. I want you to live a happy life. I pray for you everyday— I want you to know that. Even where I am now, I'm praying for you—and that must carry some extra weight because if I'm in heaven (and I certainly hope that's my destination!) then I'm a little closer to Jesus and he can hear me better. I'm not asking you to live a happy life because mine was cut short—that's stupid. I don't want my death to hold you back in any way. It's ok to be sad for me, but also be happy— after all, I had the best kid-sister in the world and now I'm in heaven where there is no more war.

There are so many things I wanted to do with you, but because our plans were changed I'm going to pass along some of

93

my wisdom (yes, I have some!). Here's my Top 10:

1. Never poke a wet cat with a stick (That's how I got the scar on my face).

2. Always check the weather report before you leave home. You know, always be prepared.

3. Read great books. Start with <u>The Count of Monte Cristo</u>, by Alexander Dumas. You won't be disappointed. All the books in my room are my favorites—I didn't waste any money on stupid literature. They are all yours now—enjoy!

4. Every once in a while, empty the dishwasher for mom. She loves it! When you start to drive, fill up the gas tank for dad. He loves that!

5. Sometimes the greatest challenges we face are little; it's not until they are over that you will understand just how important they are. Set your goals and reach them. That way you'll never have regrets. Or at least fewer regrets than most!

6. Be a good friend. It's challenging at times, but it's a lesson that carries over into everything else. If you want to have a good friend, be a good friend.

7. When you're sad, cry. When you're happy, laugh. It's simple, but people complicate it. Don't get caught up in that emotional-cover-up junk. If you feel it—feel it. Don't be shy!

8. Eat healthy food. I know I sound like mom, but after watching people in basic training nearly go through withdrawal from unhealthy food, I was grateful that I didn't have to suffer that.

9. Read your bible every day and go to Mass. If I've learned anything from being in the service, it's that we all need God. He'll never let you down.

10. Keep your room clean. Yes, I sound like mom, again, but it really does make a difference. I always liked having a clean place to sleep and read. If you need your own space—and we all do—make it a clean space. It says a great deal about the kind of person you are.

So be tough, Kit-Kat! Stay sassy. Always remember that I love you. I don't know what heaven is like but I know that God has a greater plan for his people than sadness and war. Maybe it all comes together in heaven. No, not maybe—it does!

Love you always and forever!
John Paul

Can I Manage Challenge #5?

"Courage doesn't always roar. Sometimes courage is the little voice at the end of the day that says I'll try again tomorrow."
—Mary Anne Radmacher

After finding the box, Caitlin seemed to be more like herself again. She had her gift from John Paul. On the way home from school that Monday, after picking up the mail, she suddenly stopped. "Oh my gosh! Jeff, the Circuit Challenge is next week!"

I groaned. "Don't remind me."

"I forgot all about it with everything."

"It's OK. I'll just give Frank twenty dollars and the whole thing can be over."

Caitlin eyed me carefully. "Do you have twenty dollars?"

"No."

"Then let's train. You can do it, Jeff. Don't give in to Frank just yet. Do the Challenge. I'll help."

"Caitlin, I'm not sure that's such a great idea. It's a lie. It's a bet. It's twenty dollars. Who really cares? So what if I lose the bet?"

Caitlin poked me in the chest with her finger. "You listen to me, Jefferson. Frank is a bully and he's trying to catch you in a lie."

"It *is* a lie!"

"That's not the point!"

"Then what is the point of all this? Why shouldn't I just go and tell Mr. Pullup it was all just a misunderstanding?"

"The point is that Frank shouldn't treat you the way he does. You're a good person and you wouldn't let him cheat. You're a good friend and didn't want to get Mike in trouble. I'm the one that made the bet. I believe in you. This may end up being your greatest moment."

"I don't want my greatest moment to be a Circuit Challenge."

"Why not?"

"Caitlin, it's gym class. It's a Circuit Challenge. It just doesn't feel important anymore."

"I don't understand."

"Things just feel different now. After John Paul—he gave his life for his country. *That* is a great sacrifice. His greatest moments were when he did things for you, all the time he spent with us. He left you the box. That was a great thing. I see my parents working hard to make ends meet. They sacrifice so much for us. That is a great thing. My dad practically saved your life! That was one of his greatest moments. Competing in a Circuit Challenge for something that is way out of my reach just doesn't feel important."

Caitlin looked down at her feet. "John Paul's rule number five."

"What?"

"In his letter to me. The one in the box. Rule number five." Caitlin quoted John Paul's letter, "'Sometimes the greatest challenges we face are little; it's not until they are over that you will understand just how important they were. Set your goals and reach them. That way you'll never have regrets. Or at least fewer regrets than most.'

Do you see? This is important. It's a challenge that you *can* do and so you *should*."

Could she be right? Could this little challenge be important to me later? Would I regret giving up the bet with Frank or would I regret following through and failing?

Dig Down Deep

"Sports do not build character. They reveal it."
—Heywood Broun

At 5:15 I was at the park. Caitlin had dusted off the clipboard with the basic training plan from John Paul. I ran and jumped, did 50 push-ups and 5 pull-ups. I even jumped rope 205 times before I missed. And that was just the second-first day of training. All the work we had done before had paid off.

Caitlin was jumping up and down, waving me on as I came around the last corner of the trail. "Faster, Jeff! Just a little faster!"

I dug down deep, as John Paul would have.

The next Thursday was the big Circuit Challenge. News of the bet between Frank and I had spread all over school. Frank Daring had challenged little Jefferson Stanhope to a Circuit Challenge for $20.00. Other kids started placing bets on who would win. Odds were naturally in Frank's favor.

"Don't you dare make a bet!" I warned Jabari when I saw him putting money into a pool that I would win.

"Why not?" he asked. "Caitlin said you ran really fast. She said you had a chance to win."

"Jabari, even I wouldn't place a bet that I would win."

"Come on, Jeff. Have faith."

News of the challenge had even reached Mr. Pullup's ears. "Seems you'll need a very trustworthy counter, Stanhope," he said quietly as we lined up for attendance.

"Yes, please."

He smiled. "What level will you be going for today?"

"Blue."

His eyebrows arched in surprise. "Very good. I'm assigning Chris to be your counter." Mr. Pullup leaned in and whispered, "Chris is not a favorite of Frank's, but I happen to know that he hasn't placed any bets. He'll be an honest counter for you."

As we lined up for the challenge, my nerves started to quake in my knees.

"You can do it, Jeff!" Chris said, holding the counting clipboard and stop watch ready. "Frank needs a lesson."

"I'll try."

I was lined up to do the running first. Just as well, I thought. I did my best at running. This meant, however, that the vertical jump was second to last and my legs would be tired. But I wasn't expecting to do well on that part anyway, so I didn't worry and just focused on each exercise.

I dug deep.

I faced my challenge.

I counted right along with Chris.

I heard Caitlin and Jabari[55] shouting from the door of the gym: "Dig Deep! Dig Deep!" Other kids, in the spirit of the challenge, joined in with the chant. Soon, everyone who wasn't huffing and puffing in the challenge was chanting "dig deep!" And I must admit, it felt pretty great

---

[55] They are not in my gym class, but both decided to do their best to use bathroom passes to come watch the Challenge.

to have so many people cheering me on.

Jefferson Stanhope final count:
1. Sprinting – 5 times in 1:40 min. Blue Level
2. Push-ups – 30 Blue Level
3. Stairs – 30 Green Level
4. 10 Wall Jumps – 1 at Yellow, 1 at Green, 8 at Blue
5. Pull-ups – 8 Blue Level
6. Sit-ups – 40 Blue Level

Frank Daring Final Count:
1. Sprinting – 8 times in 2:40 min. Gold Level
2. Push-ups – 50 Gold Level
3. Stairs – 60 Gold Level
4. 10 Wall Jumps – 9 at Purple; 1 at Gold
5. Pull-ups – 10 Gold Level
6. Sit-ups – 73 Purple Level

After gym class, Frank walked toward me. "Well?" Frank said. "Neither of us did it. But I was closer than you. Pay up."

"No deal. The bet was that we would complete the levels. Me at Blue. You at Gold. Since we didn't, we don't owe anyone anything."

Frank's nostrils flared[56]. "We made a bet!"

"And we both did really good, but we didn't complete the Challenge. Better luck next time." Walking away from Frank felt like turning my back on a rabid bear, but with Mr. Pullup watching and the entire gym class knowing the details of the bet, Frank did nothing.

---

[56] Gross. Especially with all the sweat dripping off the tip of his nose.

What Else Is Possible?

"Painting is just another way of keeping a diary."
—Pablo Picasso

It took two weeks to finish. Two weeks of standing in the cubby, painting. Mom let me borrow her iPod for those two weeks to help block out the sounds of conversation that drifted over the cubby walls. She downloaded some of my music, but much of hers came through, so it was mostly George Winston and the music from The Last of the Mohicans that became the soundtrack of my painting. And I liked it. The instrumental music left room for the mood; it wasn't not spoiled by lyrics. The tones, the piano, the orchestra joined my paintbrush, making each stroke of paint vibrant. When I look at my ceiling tile, I can feel the music drifting off the layers of paint into my soul.

I have new respect for Mrs. Spaglio. During my two weeks, she worked hard to keep my painting hidden. She never tried to peek at what I was doing, just visited me outside the cubby doorway and asked if I needed anything.

The idea for the tile came to me as I watched the tree fall. I thought about gravity and how it's been working against me all these years, keeping me short,[57] making the vertical jump in Circuit training nearly impossible— until I started training for it. That's when it hit me. If I don't like something, I can change it. I jumped to the Blue line in circuit. I never thought that was possible.

Now I'm wondering what else is possible.

"It's the flag," Amber said, sounding very unimpressed. "It's a tree with the leaves painted like a flag." She didn't see the shape of the tree, the one straight limb pointing west, the roots exposed with a small metal box tucked safely among its tendrils.

"No. I've seen that silhouette before," another student said. "That's from World War II."

I held up a copy of the photo from WWII and launched into my explanation. "The original photograph, taken by Joe Rosenthal, of the six men raising the flag on the island of Iwo Jima in Japan was taken on February 23rd, 1945. Of the six men, three of them died shortly after the picture was taken: Frank Sousley, Harlon Block, and Michael Strank. The three men who survived, John Bradley, Ira Hayes, and Rene Gagnon, came home as American Heroes, but according to what I've read online, all of them refused the honor, saying that only the men who never made it off that island were the heroes. The original photograph won the Pulitzer Prize and is now a bronze monument in Washington, D.C."

"But what is so original about the flag?" Amber asked.

"Because the men who formed our country did so with originality and determination. Out of a group of colonies,

---

[57] I know gravity doesn't keep me short. No one in my family is short. Just me. So I blame gravity.

they designed a country, wrote the laws and fought for freedom."

Frank scoffed. "I thought this was Art class, not History."

I thought it best to just ignore him.

"I painted the flag in the leaves because it seems that we've all forgotten where we are. Some parents complained about the National Anthem because God is mentioned in it, so we don't have an anthem anymore in school. We are supposed to love and accept everyone, but it seems to me that no one is loved and no one is hated. But that's not what our country is supposed to be. We should stand for freedom and hate oppression. We should love our God and our government, but we are told it's not politically acceptable to do either because someone might be offended. There isn't a flag in this school, there's one on the flag pole, but who notices it anymore?

"I chose to use the Iwo Jima photograph as a model because it surprised me that the men who survived were ashamed that they lived. The three survivors were called home by President Roosevelt and asked to join a Bond Tour to help raise money for the war. Back then the President couldn't just spend money on the war. The American people purchased bonds and that's what paid for the war. That surprised me, too.

"I changed the elements around the flag raising to include things from my life." I looked at Caitlin as she quickly wiped tears from her eyes. "I've never been in a war and I never want to be. I've never even seen a war movie and I don't know that I want to. I don't think movies should make war look beautiful or appealing. War is ugly and dark, but I think it's necessary. I believe that anyone who fights in a battle is a hero. The term "survivor's guilt" describes the affects soldiers or anyone that lives through a traumatic experience, feels. Guilt for living when others didn't. Guilt for not dying. All of their family members are relieved when their sons and brothers, daughters and sisters come home from war, but some of them would rather have died with their buddies. I know what it's like to be someone who loves a soldier who has died. This painting is about surviving a loss."

Amber interrupted me. "The American flag's design has been repeated again and again in art. One of the requirements of the ceiling tile contest is originality."[58]

"My ceiling tile is not the final product."

"And what is, Mr. Stanhope?" Mrs. Spaglio asked, smiling. She understood. She had known John Paul.

"The reaction the flag should have on us."

"What do you mean?" Frank asked, joining Amber in the negative questioning of my painting. Strangely, I wasn't afraid of their questions. It was just another challenge, one that I was prepared for.

"At the Fourth of July parade," I continued, "the Boy Scout troop carried the flag and the Veterans walked behind it. Some of the Veterans were too old to walk the entire parade, so they rode in a flatbed truck, but they stood in the back of that truck because the flag was before them. When they passed by, some people stood up and saluted. Other people put their hands over their heart. But most people stayed sitting on the curb or in their lawn chairs. They missed the point. The American flag is a symbol of being free, of having the right to free speech and freedom of religion. People who designed the

---

[58] As soon as she interrupted me, I realized that Amber *used to* make me so angry. A few months ago, her questioning my originality would have made me blush and go mute. Instead, I took a deep breath, relaxed my fists, dug down deep and continued as if nothing in the world bothered me.

flag and flew it hundreds of years ago fought for those freedoms. We are still fighting today. Men and women are still dying because we want to preserve freedom."

Caitlin was sitting tall and proud. She understood.

Frank scoffed. "So you want people to salute your painting?"

"I want people to remember what the flag stands for. I want to honor a fallen hero. A friend. I want to dedicate this ceiling tile to John Paul Amore. I want to put something of worth above our heads. Maybe when we pass underneath this ceiling tile we can remember the soldiers. They aren't faceless people wearing fatigues. They are people who used to walk through the halls of their school—this school. Someday we might be overseas fighting against an evil.

"Mrs. Spaglio, I don't care what grade you give me on this ceiling tile project. I just want to add the greatest symbol of freedom I know to our school. It's been missing for long enough."

I took my seat and mentally blocked out the rest of the unveilings. I didn't care what anyone else had painted. Speaking freely in front of the class had drained me completely. All I wanted to do was go home and sleep, but there were two more classes to go.

The Contest

"Planning means nothing if you are not prepared accept the unexpected." —*Author Unknown*

One month later, all the eighth graders in Art class had finished their ceiling tiles. For two days, all the tiles were hung in the hallway between the main office and the gym.[59] Parents and students were invited back to school Friday at 4:00 for the gallery showing. Cookies, punch and coffee were served as the judges walked up and down the hallway, looking up at the tiles and down at their clip board.

It was unnerving.

I watched each judge as they assessed my painting. One clearly loved it. The other two were more stoic in their judging. If my mom was a judge, I would have won immediately.

When the judging was over, Mrs. Spaglio asked all the students to stand under their ceiling tiles. She talked on the P.A. system for a few moments about the importance

---

[59] Mrs. Spaglio likes to have them all together for the judges, which means Mr. Moppet has a big job for the week leading up to the contest deadline. He takes out all the tiles from last year and puts up the new ones. Mrs. Spaglio knows how much work this is and helps. She also treats Mr. Moppet and his wife to a dinner at a nice restaurant as a way to say, "thank you and I'm sorry for your back ache."

of art and the high quality forms of expression she has seen this year. She encouraged parents to take us to art museums and enroll us in summer art classes, anything to keep our interest and desire for art alive.

"And now for the winners of this year's ceiling tile contest. There are no monetary prizes, but I do have a certificate of participation for each of you. I can guarantee a place in the advanced Art class at the high school next year for the two students who received the highest scores.

"I know you are all anxious to hear the results. Let me just say,[60] that I am very proud of each of you. To be an artist is to put a piece of your soul on display for others to judge. It's never easy. You've done well. Two of you have done exceedingly well. In fact, there was a tie. Two perfect scores. And I can't think of two better students to receive this honor. Caitlin Amore and Jefferson Stanhope. Congratulations."

My mom screamed with joy.

Dad hooted.[61]

George patted me on the back.

Amelia hugged me.[62]

When I finally extracted myself from my family, Mrs. Spaglio had us come forward to receive our gold-sealed certificates and a slip of paper for Art class admission next year. We stood together. Friends. Good friends. Great friends who shared a loss and found a buried treasure.

---

[60] Another stall. We all moaned with anticipation. Mrs. Spaglio was obviously enjoying this.

[61] Yeah, it was super embarrassing.

[62] That was a first.

Gravity's Final Revenge

"Every day is an opportunity to make a new happy ending."
—Author Unknown

We lingered.

My mom can talk with anyone. And she did. As the mother of two previously inept artists of ceiling tiles, she was really enjoying the moment, talking with her hands, smiling, laughing. That joy is from the ceiling tile, my painting. That joy on her face, in the way she is talking, is my joy.

Mr. Moppet doesn't know the joy of a painted ceiling tile. To him, these are burdens. To him, the annual ceiling tile contest is a battle of strength and balance versus gravity and ladder hauling. He started moving a few ceiling tiles to make room for the winning tiles before the families started leaving. I didn't blame him; it was Friday after all. I'm sure he wanted to be home and off his feet. We were down the hall and plenty far away from any hazard the ladder might impose, so Mr. Retsim agreed that Mr. Moppet could start.

Mom and Mrs. Amore agreed that the occasion called for a celebration beyond punch and cookies and certificates. They had already left to go to the store to buy barbeque fixings when I heard the crash. I didn't have to look. I knew. I could tell by the sound. It was just my luck. It sounded like my kind of gravity: heavy and chalky with a splash of spite.

Mr. Moppet was not hurt.

My ceiling tile was in pieces.

Gravity had returned to exact its revenge on me. I had denounced gravity for my height and overcome its effect on me during the Circuit Challenge. It had returned with a vengeance. Mr. Moppet had dropped my ceiling tile.

He stood there, on the third rung of the ladder, staring at the remains of my masterpiece. Mrs. Spaglio ran to the dusty pieces and immediately began to reassemble them.

I felt sick.

All that work.

Gone.

In an instant, the work was gone.

My feet were glued to the spot as I stared at the mess.

"Come on," Caitlin said, taking me by the hand.

"I can't look."

"I'll help," she gently pulled me along. "I'll help."

It didn't look too bad at first. We all kneeled and put the pieces together; one giant, dusty puzzle. Only seven pieces.

"Can we glue them together?" Caitlin asked.

Mr. Moppet shook his head. "Wouldn't risk it. It might come apart and then it would fall on someone." He rubbed his neck. "I'm sure sorry. Just slipped right out of my hands."

"It's ok," I said.[63]

"What if we glue it to a large piece of wood?" Mrs. Spaglio suggested. "Would that work?"

Mr. Amore shook his head. "Too heavy. It poses the same risk of falling as gluing it does."

"But we can glue it to a piece of wood," Caitlin said.

---

[63] It wasn't, but I didn't know what else to say.

110

"Your dad just said," I started, but Caitlin wasn't looking at me or the broken tile. Mrs. Spaglio followed her gaze.

"Brilliant!" Mrs. Spaglio clapped her hands together. "Oh, Caitlin! You're brilliant."

Caitlin beamed.

Mr. Amore, dad, Mr. Moppet and I weren't following. "Why is Caitlin brilliant?" her dad asked.

"We'll glue it together," Caitlin said, "and it can go in the showcase with the trophies."

Right across the hall from the main office was a twenty-foot long showcase with all the athletic awards from the past thirty years. It took some convincing on Mrs. Spaglio's part, but Mr. Retsim finally agreed. My ceiling tile was glued together on a large piece of plywood and put on display in the showcase. Granted, it was behind the trophies but still visible. The best part was that no one had to look up to see it.

Epilogue

"Happiness does not come from doing easy work, but from the afterglow of satisfaction that comes after the achievement of a difficult task that demanded our best." —Theodore Rubin

Next to my glued painting in the trophy case, Mr. Retsim added two framed pictures of John Paul: one was his eighth grade school picture and the other was his picture in uniform. The dates of his birth and death were included.

I didn't get an 'A' in gym class, even though I had almost passed the Blue level. I got an 'A-'. It was enough to qualify for the golf team and I spent the next year only carrying my own golf clubs and not serving as caddy for the whole team.

Frank Daring finally started shaving and his fuzzy mustache was gone for a while. By the end of our first day of high school, he had a five o-clock shadow and an ego to match.

Caitlin and I are still best friends. I asked to go with her and her parents to church the Sunday after John Paul's funeral. I've been going every Sunday. I like the

112

Catholic Church. The traditions make sense to me and the incense has become a source of comfort and meaning—and sneezing—but I don't mind. My parents are happy that I've found a faith that I understand. They come with us sometimes and dad said that if I wanted to become Catholic, he would attend the classes with me.

George is still an idiot, but he leaves for college next year, so we've called a truce. Ever since John Paul's funeral, he doesn't pick on me as much. That is a little bit of good.

Mom quit her minimum wage job and started working with dad at the copy machine business. She told him that if she was going to work to help the family, the best thing she could do was to support her husband and make his business thrive. It's working. Within six months of mom joining Dad's business, there was too much work for them to handle and they hired back one of dad's former employees.

I'm still short, but I grew almost three inches over the summer.

With the family business doing so well, Dad bought an old car for Amelia so she wouldn't be forgotten at practice anymore. I still don't have a cell phone, but I don't mind. Everything else is good.

It is true that you can find a pot of gold at the end of a rainbow. It might not be made of real gold, but it's value is beyond belief.

A Note from Jessica Schaub

I hope you enjoyed meeting Jefferson and Caitlin. They are very dear to my heart and their story, while fictional, I believe accounts for many friendships and our childhood neighborhood friends.

Much of this book was generated from my own childhood memories. My junior high gym class had circuit training on Tuesdays and Thursdays, and my 8th grade Art Project was to paint a ceiling tile. It was a horrible painting and deserved the dark spot near the emergency exit by the science rooms. If you go to my middle school, the painting is gone. Only real legacies last forever. I am no Michelangelo, but I hope this story leaves a print on the ceiling of your heart.

This book is a venture from my typical writing styles. While many of the professionals will advice that a writer should write one genre only, I don't. I don't like one type of pizza, I love variety in all forms, and that is reflected in my writing.

If you, like me, enjoy different types of books, I invite you to explore my other books. They can be found at any bookstore and online.

Unforgettable Roads

Gateways, Book I of The Elemental Chronicles

The Elder's Circle, Book II of The Elemental Chronicles

If you enjoyed *Gravity*, I thank you in advance for leaving a review on your favorite book review website. There's

Amazon, Goodreads, Smashwords to name a few. Reviews for authors are the best presents ever!

God Bless!

Jessica Schaub

To read an interview with Jessica Schaub, visit
https://www.smashwords.com/profile/view/jessicaschaub

64608140R00070